D0408376

A
BAKER STREET
WEDDING

A
BAKER STREET
WEDDING

MICHAEL ROBERTSON

MINOTAUR BOOKS
A THOMAS DUNNE BOOK
New York

A THOMAS DUNNE BOOK FOR MINOTAUR BOOKS
An imprint of St. Martin's Press

A BAKER STREET WEDDING. Copyright © 2018 by Michael Robertson. All rights reserved. Printed in the United States of America. For information, address St. Martin's Press, 175 Fifth Avenue, New York, N.Y. 10010.

www.thomasdunnebooks.com
www.minotaurbooks.com

The Library of Congress Cataloging-in-Publication Data is available upon request.

ISBN 978-1-250-06007-5 (hardcover)
ISBN 978-1-4668-6528-0 (ebook)

Our books may be purchased in bulk for promotional, educational, or business use. Please contact your local bookseller or the Macmillan Corporate and Premium Sales Department at 1-800-221-7945, extension 5442, or by email at MacmillanSpecialMarkets@macmillan.com.

First Edition: December 2018

10 9 8 7 6 5 4 3 2 1

This book is dedicated to Marcia Markland, my first editor (without her early encouragement, even the first book in this series would not have been written), and to Rebecca Oliver, my first agent (without her efforts, the series would not have been financially possible). I am deeply grateful to them both.

ACKNOWLEDGMENTS

My thanks to Nettie Finn, for an extremely helpful and insightful edit, and to the staff at Minotaur: jacket designer David Baldeosingh Rotstein; marketer Martin Quinn; production manager Eva Diaz; production editor Elizabeth Curione; publicist Kayla Janas; and copy editor Carol Edwards.

BAKER STREET
WEDDING

Prologue

Laura Penobscott was too tall. Not just taller than all the fourteen-year-old boys at the Bodfyn boarding school dance, which might have been regarded as quite temporary and soon to be adjusted in the natural biological timing of things, but taller than all the other fourteen-year-old girls, as well. Even as tall as Mrs. Hatfield.

And she was not athletically tall, which would have made it all right perhaps. She wasn't good at volleyball. She was just plain gangly.

Scarecrow. The gangliness and the red hair, and the mix of freckles and acne, and the uncorrected gap in the front teeth—in the process of being corrected right now, in fact, with the necessary shiny hardware—accounted for that nickname.

She wasn't sure whether the boys had started that nickname or the girls. It wasn't the first, or worst, nickname that anyone had ever thrown at her—after all, her surname was Penobscott and she had been in the third grade once—but none of those had stuck. Someone had thought up "Scarecrow" for her earlier this year, though, just prior to Halloween, and that one did take hold. "Laura, go as a scarecrow," everyone had said, with giggles.

And so she had. But not just *a* scarecrow—*the* scarecrow. With straw stuffed in her sleeves, a floppy hat, and the flopping arms—which somehow she had been able to mimic perfectly the very first time she saw it on the telly—she had gone as the scarecrow from *The Wizard of Oz*.

And every chance she got at that Halloween party, she had flapped her straw arms, opened her eyes wide, gazed directly at whoever had unwittingly supplied the conversational opportunity, put an index finger to her temple, and said, "Oh if I only had a brain!"

And everyone got the joke. Because everyone knew Laura Penobscott had a brain. She was even smarter than she was tall. And at the Halloween party, they learned she also had the ability to mimic not having one when she chose to. She could mimic anything, at the drop of a floppy hat.

But brains don't count for much at dance parties, and neither does mimicry, unless you're making cruel fun of someone, which Laura declined to do. Laura and her two best female friends were now at the Winter Holiday Dance.

They were standing just a few feet away from the punch bowl, but not right at the punch bowl, because they knew enough not to put themselves in a position where other fourteen-year-old girls could later say that Laura, Lisa, and Lilly, the three Ls, never got asked to dance, but just stood all night at the punch bowl. If they didn't stand right there, no one could take a picture to prove it.

Most of the boys were just standing around, as well, in groups of three or four along the opposite wall, talking to one another with great animation, and laughing gratuitously, very much self-aware. It was all a show, Laura knew. Or at least suspected. Occasionally, one of them would throw side glances at the girls on the other side, and in the meantime they would stare at the girls the other boys had already decided were pretty enough to take onto the dance floor.

The dance party had proper chaperones. A female teacher, Mrs. Hatfield, of the music and theater department, stood at the front, trying to look current, but with an eye out for inappropriate skirt lengths and other things that adults thought might inspire trouble.

A male teacher, Mr. Turner, of the social sciences department, stood guard at the back exit, in case any juvenile might try to sneak out for a cig or some other activity resembling juvenile mischief. He pushed his unruly brown hair back, and kept a wary eye on one particular boy—the alpha, clearly—in the popular group, who was talking and gesturing with more athletic authority than the rest.

Laura Penobscott looked in the direction of that boy herself (though only for an instant, she was sure), and she sighed. She already knew. He wasn't going to come over. He had glanced in her direction more than once since entering the room, but he wasn't going to come over. He was only going to go for one of the girls deemed eligible enough to be on the dance floor already. Of course that's how it was. After all, he was a boy.

It was a disappointed sigh, because Laura already understood that's how things worked, but it wasn't a worried sigh. Perhaps it was because someone had told her that her long legs, which seemed like stilts now, were going to get a much better reaction from the boys a bit further on.

Or perhaps she simply knew that she would get along just fine either way.

"You will be a star, young lady," Mrs. Hatfield had told her in drama class. "In life, where it counts. Because of what's inside you. All the rest is just by the way."

In any case, Laura sighed only slightly at the athletic boy's indifference, and now one of her girlfriends nudged her.

Another boy—not from one of the groups along the wall, but one who had been standing by himself over by the door—was now in motion. He was coming in the direction of the three Ls. And his laser-focused gaze— whenever he looked up from his own feet as he nervously made sure he put one of them in front of the other—was on Laura.

It was "Haughty Bobby." Or "Potty Bobby," said one of Laura's girlfriends. He had been known by both names, but it was the second one that stuck.

Laura didn't know what his surname was. None of the students did. For most of them, it had been much more fun to call him by invented names—he was just much too easy a target. On the very first day of school, before anyone's names were known, a couple of his peers had tried "Pizza Face" on him, because of both his size and complexion. But that hadn't stuck, because it was already taken. One or two "Pizza Face" students had already been established in the previous term, and they were still around.

So then they moved on to calling him Haughty, because he didn't socialize much (no one much cared why) and wasn't good at any sport except cannonball splashing in the pool.

But then came the name that stayed. Potty Bobby was for a public episode or two of flatulence.

Now, Potty Bobby lost his nerve at the last moment, stumbling over his own Doc Martens at the dance. Laura's friends giggled. Bobby, red-faced and humiliated, tried to pretend that he was, in fact, just heading to the punch bowl. He flailed for it like a drowning man grasping for the side of a boat.

Laura's girlfriends giggled some more, quite openly.

That's enough of that, thought Laura. She shot a look that said so to her friends, and then she walked over to the punch bowl.

5

"Would you pour a cup for me, too, please?" she said.

Potty Bobby turned to look—saw with amazement who had spoken to him—and broke out in an instant sweat.

"I . . . I . . . yes," he stammered.

"I'm always so clumsy at these things," said Laura as the boy handed her a paper cup filled, rather inexactly, with oversweetened red punch. "It's nice to find someone who can fill a cup without spilling much."

The boy nodded, not quite able to speak.

"My name's Laura," she said.

"B-B-B-Bobby!"

The way he said his name was like a rock song Laura had heard on the radio—"Bad to the Bone." B-b-b-b-baaa-aad. Baaa-aad-to-the-bone Bobby was what occurred to her, which was quite funny, but she managed to keep it to herself and not even let the thought of it show in her eyes. She just smiled, and waited patiently as Bobby struggled for something to say next.

His eyes were wide like a deer's as he looked at her, and the sweat was literally pouring from his face. He desperately grabbed a handful of cocktail napkins.

And now the music was starting up again. A slow dance.

Dear God.

Potty Bobby stared at her in wide-eyed alarm.

Without even turning, Laura knew that her friends were starting to giggle again.

That's just too bad, thought Laura.

She held out her hand. An astonished and terrified Bobby took that cool hand palm-down in his own damp one and stumbled with Laura onto the dance floor.

Along the wall, the athletic boy who couldn't make up his mind whether his social status could withstand asking Laura to dance glanced in their direction with a puzzled look, but Laura took no notice. She hadn't done it to make him jealous.

The song was a slow lament about teenage years from Janis Ian. Not a cheerier one from Echosmith that Laura would like many years later as an adult.

Blue, pink, and yellow crepe-paper streamers cast shadows from the slightly dimmed gymnasium ceiling lamps; an overhead sequined attempt at a disco ball rotated in fits and starts. Potty Bobby's shoes made squeaky sounds when he tried to shuffle his feet on the floor. Laura's girlfriends on the sidelines continued to giggle. The gentle, sad music seemed to go on forever.

And then, just as it reached the last refrain, Potty Bobby suddenly lurched in close to Laura.

With his sweaty cheek against hers, he whispered, "I'm going to be a spy."

"What?"

"I've given it quite a lot of thought. I have all the skills."

"Oh?" said Laura. She managed not to laugh. Or to take a napkin to the transferred sweat on her cheek.

She'd had plenty of guidance, and much discussion

with her friends beforehand, on how to talk to boys at a party. This topic had not come up. She went with her own very clear sense of logic, and said simply, "Why do you want to do that?"

"Because of what they do."

"Do you know what spies do?" she asked.

"Of course. They dress well and play baccarat, and they know all about wines, and they have guns, and fast cars, and fast—"

He stopped and blushed.

"Women," said Laura, finishing the sentence for him, and this time she couldn't help but laugh.

"But you're talking about MI6 and James Bond, I think," she added quickly. "I thought you meant the other kind of spy."

"There's another kind?"

"The people who become spies because they grow up mad at the culture they live in, and so they think betrayal would be heroic. Or because they meet someone from the other side who they think is sexy. Or because someone offers them a lot of money. Or someone blackmails them. Those kinds of spies—well, I don't think they have a lot of fun, and anyway, it's no way to impress girls."

Now Potty Bobby stared at Laura with an expression of great disappointment. He seemed so totally at a loss that she wondered if perhaps she should have said nothing at all.

But then he said, "I'll be a zombie killer, then."

"A what?"

"A zombie killer. I mean, a killer of zombies. Not . . . a zombie who kills. A zombie killer like in the video games."

"There are no zombies," said Laura. "And what kind of ambition is it to be a killer of anything?"

"Oh," said Potty Bobby, and then he went quiet for a long moment.

"You know what someone told me?" she said before the silence could become any more awkward.

"No," said Bobby. Then, quite sincerely, he added, "I don't eavesdrop."

"Someone told me," said Laura, "that I am very young—and that means you are, too, of course—and that it is impossible to know in this moment how young we are, and that every trouble we have, no matter how great and terrifying and hopeless it seems now, is purely temporary and that we will overcome it and find a future that we could not even have imagined."

"Really?"

"Yes."

Potty Bobby thought about that.

"Perhaps I won't be a zombie killer."

"Good."

"I'll be a magnet."

"What?"

"A magnet."

"Oh," said Laura after a moment of pondering. "You'll

be a magnate! A person who through hard work and perseverance and perhaps a little luck becomes very rich and powerful in some particular industry!"

Laura had to remind herself now not to sound like a dictionary when explaining something. But it was perhaps excusable, she thought, given how seldom the word had come up in conversation.

"Yes," said Bobby. "I'll be a magnate."

"Brilliant!" said Laura.

But now Bobby went silent again, and Laura was afraid that she might have pushed him beyond either his emotional or conversational limits—until she realized that he had stopped because he was staring at something over her shoulder.

She turned to look.

Behind her was—well, nothing unusual, as far she could tell. Nothing that should have caused this adolescent with a huge crush on her to look away suddenly. Look down at his own feet in shyness perhaps, but not ignore her and look away.

Perhaps it was the chaperones? Laura looked around to see.

Mrs. Hatfield was still at the entrance door, checking someone's hem length, but Mr. Turner, at the exit, did seem to have an eye in their direction.

Laura had an impulse to cuddle up a bit to her shy dance partner just to annoy the chaperones, but she didn't. There was no telling what that might do to Bobby.

And then, quite unexpectedly, it was Bobby himself who leaned in.

Laura braced herself. His right cheek was pressed against her right cheek. His mouth was nearing her ear!

"Thank you," he said.

And then there was a sudden and blinding flash of light. When the green and yellow and red spots finally stopped flashing in Laura's eyes, she knew what had happened: Laura Penobscott had been caught by the yearbook photographer, slow-dancing cheek-to-cheek with the most embarrassing boy in the school!

1

TWENTY YEARS LATER

A young woman ran across Bodfyn Moor just after dusk, with the sun gone and the quarter moon not yet risen. The white-gray rocks, embedded everywhere in the thawing mud and unseen until she struck them, punished her feet painfully, but she did not slow until she reached the top of a small rise.

She had to stop, just for a moment, because her lungs were heaving and burning. She looked behind her for her pursuers. She could not see them in the pitch-dark, nor could she hear them clearly, with the wind howling and whipping the heather about. But she was sure they were there.

The young woman had crow's-feet and shadows around her eyes, but they were not real. They were due to an especially heavy application of Ben Nye eye makeup for the stage. Her face was lined, but the wrinkles were drawn in with a pencil. She had ruby red lips, but they were not her preferred color. And she had blood on her hands—which was advertised as tasting like peppermint, and resistant to melting under the sweat of stage lights, but easily removable with warm soap and water, unlike the blood on the hands of the character she had been cast to play.

What was real about the young woman was her jet black hair, her startling blue-violet eyes, and her very sincere desire to be an actress—and now, her very real fear of what was pursuing her.

Her parents had once told her that she could be the next Elizabeth Taylor. And after she had Googled Elizabeth Taylor, she knew that was a compliment. But, of course, she wanted to be like Scarlett Johansson. Or like Katie Holmes. Or like the tall, famously freckled Laura Rankin. Being like any of them would do.

She was young and healthy and forward-looking, and she did not believe in curses, despite what the others back at the theater rehearsal had said. A brisk walk on the moor, with the wind blowing and Wagner playing loudly in her headphones, would clear her mind, help her ignore all the nonsense, and also help put her many lines into a context all her own.

The walk had begun pleasantly enough. With headphones on, she couldn't hear the gusting wind, but she could see it—whipping the pink heather, stirring the early-spring grass. She saw patches of tall yellow gorse bushes moving in the wind, as well, and she picked her way around them; one had to avoid their thorns.

The wind stirred no dust—it was the moor, after all, not a desert, and except for the white-gray rocks, everything there was either living or had been.

She had hiked to the top of the nearest hill on Bodfyn Moor and paused, leaning against a granite tor that had withstood eons of weather, and hoping to see a couple of the wild ponies known to frequent the region. But no—not this time. In the waning light, she had seen only a large patch of head-high yellow gorse, the yellow flowers shifting and shimmering in the last ray of sun, and the branches still moving in the wind.

Which was odd. Because everywhere else the wind had stopped. The heather nearby didn't seem to be moving at all.

She took off her headphones to listen, not trusting her vision alone.

Yes, the wind had stopped.

And yet the branches of the nearest yellow gorse bush she had just passed, only a few yards behind her, had just now moved again. She was sure of it; and not only was she sure she had seen that motion but now she could also smell it—the yellow gorse, when disturbed, emitted a very distinct aroma, like coconut oil—could smell it as strongly as if someone had opened a bottle of tanning lotion.

Now it was so dark that it was certainly time to head back. She wanted to walk right back down the way she had come up, using the faint gray shapes of the rocks to guide her steps.

But that would take her right by that tall patch of gorse. And she wanted to be sure.

"Hello?"

She felt foolish calling out. But she could not think of what had moved those bushes if a person had not.

"Is someone there?"

She took a tentative step in that direction—if she could be certain that no one was there, hiding behind the thorny branches, she was going to rush right past that stand of gorse and down the slope. As dark as the night now was, she would run down the path, and if her feet hit the rocks and she tripped, so be it—she would eventually get to the safety of the theater.

But now, as she took that step, the branches moved again—she heard them, smelled them, nearly felt them— and she heard a low, guttural, and frighteningly angry human sound.

She abandoned her plan. She turned and began to run farther out onto the moor.

And then, suddenly, she pitched forward. She put her arms out but found nothing to catch and break her fall. It was just all blackness. The surprise of it was so great that she could not even think to scream.

2

At the Wayward Pony, the only pub in Bodfyn, the establishment's owner had laid out a tabloid newspaper, open to the gossip pages, as he tended bar. The London-based actress Laura Rankin was getting married, and her choice of mates was a subject of discussion.

"*The Daily Sun* calls him 'the balmy barrister of Baker Street,'" said Charlie with some authority as he drew another pint for a customer. "Something to do with letters that he gets. And says he almost blew up the sewer under Hyde Park once."

Charlie, in his mid-thirties, with the slightly stocky and somewhat paunchy build of a former athlete, set the freshly filled glass on the bar with more emphasis than was really necessary.

"Says here he's a QC, though. Queen's Counsel," said a man in a wool cap, picking up the beer.

"So what?" said Charlie. "I'll bet you could throw a rock in any direction from the Inns of Court and bonk one of those."

Sophie, the barmaid, came over now. She was boisterous and several years younger than the man pouring the beer. "Oh, you're so right, Charlie," she said, laughing. "I'd have bonked one or two myself when I visited London last year. But they're all so stuffy!"

Charlie laughed, too, but halfheartedly. Of all the people in the pub, he seemed the most genuinely unhappy about the announced nuptials.

"Yes," he said. "She could have had a real man, not some toff."

Now an older man, with deliberately unkempt, Ensteinishly wild, gray hair, reached across the bar, and slapped a consoling hand on the bartender's shoulder.

"Let it go, lad," he said. "She was never for you. Fate had other things in mind."

"I know celebrities are no affair of mine, Mr. Turner," said Charlie. He still called the older man that, just as he had back in the day when Mr. Turner had been one of his teachers. "But that reminds me of a girl I knew in school. That one who, if you hadn't interrupted us when you did that time out back of the football field on the moor—"

Another man, about Charlie's age, slapped the bar and loudly said, "If he hadn't, that bird would have put a knee in your groin, Charlie! Just like all the others do!"

Everyone laughed. Charlie turned away, and as a distraction, he went to the other end of the bar, where the barmaid was polishing up a bit, and indicated that she had missed a spot.

"Don't worry, Charlie." She smiled as she took a swipe at the alleged spot, and then walked past him. "I won't knee you in the groin. Been there, done that."

There was more laughter. Charlie pretended that he had something more important to do in the back kitchen.

The barmaid drew a pint and went to put it down, very closely, in front of a dark-haired fortyish man, who stood out a bit from the others in the bar because he was wearing not only a glued-on salt-and-pepper beard but also a medieval tunic. The barmaid whispered to him as she delivered his beer, though not so softly that it could have been much of a secret.

"See you after?"

"It might be late, Sophie," said the man, in a bit of humble bragging, due to his having the lead role at the community theater. "Last week of rehearsal and all that, you know."

"It might be getting late here, too, luv," said Sophie, and she turned away with an attitude that should have made the costumed man consider that she was getting annoyed at his lack of commitment. But he quickly shrugged that thought away, because the front door had opened, admitting a blast of cold wind, which rustled the pages of the tabloid. He turned to look, hoping that a specific one of three young witches—or perhaps, in his most ambitious imagination, even all three of them in a group—had entered in need of a brew and some theatrical advice.

But no. It was only the director—a smallish, balding man in his fifties—and Mrs. Hatfield, the artistic director, who called out loudly to everyone in the pub, "Has anyone seen my Lady Macbeth?"

Everyone caught the urgency in her voice, and they all turned to look. The costumed actor shook his head.

Mrs. Hatfield proceeded to the back of the pub, where the barmaid was setting a basket of fish and chips down in front of the local real estate agent and his wife.

"Have you?" said Mrs. Hatfield, looking at each of them.

All three shook their heads.

"No," said the barmaid. "Sorry. Was she expected to be here?"

"No," said Mrs. Hatfield. "She was expected to be back at rehearsal. She went out for a walk behind the theater to center herself and recover her character's motivation. Or so she said. But that was forty minutes ago."

"So she went for a walk on the moor," said the estate agent. "She's done that before, hasn't she?"

"She's not from around here," said Mrs. Hatfield. "She's a city girl; she only came out to do the play. And she never takes this long."

At the far end of the bar, a man of about eighty, grizzled and weather-worn, put down his beer and said, "There's worse things than spending a night on the moor. It's not so bad in springtime. I got caught out at night more than once as a lad, when I had to chase down stray sheep." He picked up his beer again, and then quickly added, "And no smart remarks out of you, Charlie."

Charlie had just now come back in from the kitchen.

Now the costumed man stood, full of self-importance.

"Mrs. Hatfield, I'll help you look, if you like," he announced. "Charlie, lend us a torch? We'll find her in no time."

"I'm sure you will," said the barmaid.

"I'll help," said Mr. Turner, grabbing his raincoat.

The director stayed at the bar and shook his head as the party of three went out the door.

"Amateurs," he muttered. "Amateurs. How can anyone work like this?"

3

The next morning on Bodfyn Moor was clear and cold. Nice for visibility, but not so much for the coroner, who had to drive out from Amesbury, because Bodfyn was too small to have a coroner or constables of its own.

The coroner from Amesbury, in his fifties and standing well over six feet, had driven out willingly enough, but he already had a runny nose and scratchy throat, and now he had to get a handkerchief from his pocket to try to keep the stuff from dripping into his thick reddish brown mustache and freezing there.

He was looking down from the top of one of the moor's granite quarries at the deep, dark pool of water below. He supposed that the constables couldn't be too comfortable, either. One of them was having to squeeze into a wet suit now to go in and retrieve the body.

A small search party, perhaps slightly inebriated, had

gone out from the pub the night before, or so the coroner was told. But they had found no sign in the immediate vicinity where the hiker started out. And then, at the break of dawn, before a team of professionals could even assemble, a couple of bird-spotters had called in the bad news. That always seemed to be the way. It was always a toss-up, on the moor, whether the annual dead hiker— that seemed to be the average, one a year or so—would be found first by pensioners with cameras and binoculars pursuing yellow warblers, or by anglers pursuing brown trout. For some reason, people who had specific objectives on the moor seemed to get in less trouble than those who were merely wandering around. Especially those wandering around with headsets.

This one, a young woman, seemed to have panicked at dusk, realized that she was farther out on the moor than she intended, gotten turned around, and hurried in the wrong direction—right over the edge of the quarry.

The coroner shook his head. She wasn't the first to have done that. He doubted she would be the last. Bloody damn iPhones.

It took until midmorning for the team to finish their work. They were on foot—the area was not accessible by car—and the closest parking they had found happened to be within sight of the town's one and only pub. By the time the coroner and his team came walking back across the moor, word had gotten around.

On the outdoor deck in back of the Wayward Pony, a

crowd had gathered at the coin-operated telescope that was normally used only by tourists looking for wild ponies. But Mrs. Hatfield was looking through it now, with the other pub regulars huddled in next to her.

"Oh dear," she said. "Oh dear." She had seen what the two constables were carrying on their stretcher, and now, clearly upset, she turned away.

"What? What is it? What did you see?" asked everyone around her.

Mrs. Hatfield wiped her eyes.

"Body bag," she said.

"What? Let me see that," said Charlie, and he took command of the telescope. Then he said, "Blast. Anyone got another pound?"

"I always told you that you should have made it just ten pence," said the barmaid.

"Here's one," said the actor who had volunteered the night before, as he handed Charlie a coin. "But let us all have a look, if you don't mind."

"I'll pass," said Mr. Turner. He turned away, heading back into the pub, and now Charlie seemed to have seen enough, as well.

"Aye," he said. "Getting a bit morbid, if you ask me." He put the pound coin in, relinquished the telescope to the actor, and went back into the pub himself. He saw that there was no need to draw anyone another pint—Mr. Turner had left, and everyone else was still on the back deck.

Charlie thought it was a shame about the girl, but he

hardly knew her, and he still had something else on his mind. He walked over to the bar, retrieved the copy of *The Daily Sun* that they had all been looking at the day before, drew a pint for himself, and unfolded the paper once again on the bar. He stared at the engagement photo of Laura Rankin, sighed, and took a long draft of the beer.

4

LONDON, THREE DAYS LATER

Final rehearsals go badly as often as not. Laura knew this from hard experience in Covent Garden, and she knew it didn't apply just to theatrical premieres. She tried to keep that in mind this foggy, chilly morning in London—after the unmitigated disaster of her own wedding rehearsal.

Bugger. She was trying to sneak into Baker Street Chambers through the back entrance on the alley. She had been assured that the door would be unlocked. She tried it again, and it still didn't turn. She began to bang on the door with her fist, and then stopped. She looked both ways, up and down the alley. Had anyone seen her? Apparently not. Heard her? She hoped not. There was still no one in sight. The fog helped a little perhaps, but she knew a crowd of paparazzi was gathered at the front of the building, with eyes and ears wide open, and probably with listening devices, as well. She could not afford a ruckus.

She pounded again, but more softly.

Suddenly, the latch turned and the door opened from the inside. A white-haired, gray-uniformed security guard, close to eighty years of age, looked out apologetically at Laura.

"Sorry, miss. Meant to get to it earlier. Had a distraction," said Mr. Hendricks.

Laura stepped quickly inside, and he closed the door behind her. The man seemed just a bit out of breath, and she worried now that she had rushed him.

"Mr. Hendricks, are you all right?"

"Yes, yes, quite," he said, though Laura could tell his adrenaline was up, his blue eyes gleaming. He leaned in and whispered, "Thought a couple of them had sneaked through the lobby by tailgating the bank employees who had passes. But turns out they were just the usual misguided tourists, not paparazzi at all. I caught them in the lift and directed them to the Sherlock Holmes museum down the street, and then came straightaway for you."

"Brilliant," said Laura. "Thank you so very much."

"Now, you know you can't take the lift yourself," said Hendricks. "You'd be seen. I'll escort you up the stairs."

"No, Mr. Hendricks. You'll go back to your desk and catch your breath."

"I still run Regents Park every Saturday, miss. All the way around."

"Yes, but I'd much prefer it if you just glare out at the paparazzi for me and keep them at bay."

"As you wish," said Hendricks. He opened the stairwell door for her, smiled, and said, "Try not to get too winded yourself."

Laura wasn't sure what he meant by that, though he seemed to have actually winked. How much did he know? She decided not to ask; she let the door close behind her and hurried up the stairs.

On the second floor, she opened the stairwell door onto the stone-still legal chambers of Reggie Heath, QC.

She hurried toward Reggie's private office, her footsteps echoing on the hardwood floors. She tried his door—locked. Good, that was as it should be. She went to the receptionist's desk and picked up the phone. She needed a landline; the paparazzi were getting far too sophisticated about digital communications. She looked about once again to be sure that no one else was on the floor, and she glanced quickly at the lift to be sure no one was on the way up. No one was.

She picked up the phone and punched in a number. As it began to ring, she thought she heard a board creak at the far end of the office floor, and stood to look—but she saw nothing, and now someone had picked up at the other end of the line.

"I'm ready," said Laura happily and conspiratorially into the phone. "Are you?"

Laura laughed at the response she heard on the other end of the line—but now she heard a chime, and she looked and saw that the lift had come up to her floor. It was directly across from where she was standing, and the doors were about to open.

"Have to run," she said into the phone.

She hung up the phone just as the doors opened. When she saw who it was, she and the man in the lift both spoke at the same time, and both with a tone of disappointment.

"Oh. It's you," said Mr. Rafferty, a slight man wearing gold wire-rim glasses and an impeccable gray suit.

"Oh. It's you," said Laura.

"I thought perhaps Mr. Heath was here," said Rafferty. "Have you seen him today?"

"No," said Laura, "that would be bad luck." And then she thought to ask, "Which one were you looking for?"

"Reggie. Or Nigel, for that matter. Either one would do. Things are piling up, as you can see."

He pointed to make sure that she did see, but he wasn't indicating the shelf where the clerk would deposit incoming briefs for the barristers. There were, in fact, no briefs on the shelf. He was pointing instead at a stack of open envelopes and letters on the receptionist's desk.

"Oh," said Laura, looking. "Well, neither of them is here. And it may be a while."

"I see," said Rafferty, with a look that made it an accusation.

"There's no point in being a scold, Mr. Rafferty," said Laura in response. "I know all about the letters and your rules and Reggie's responsibilities. But everyone deserves a life. Even my fiancé."

"It's still on, then? I thought I read something in the papers, that perhaps—"

"No." Laura smiled. "Sorry if it creates an inconvenience, but Reggie and I are still getting married." And then she pointedly added, "I trust you will let that information go no further."

"Of course," said Rafferty. "I mean, of course not."

"Was there anything else, Mr. Rafferty?" asked Laura. He was still standing there in front of the lift, he was delaying her, and she spoke in a tone that she rarely had to use.

"No, ma'am . . . miss . . . missus . . . Ms. Rankin—no, thank you," said Rafferty, pressing the lift button the whole time. Now, mercifully, the doors opened, he stepped in, and he nodded to Laura as they closed again.

Laura watched the lights on the panel until she was satisfied that the lift had returned Mr. Rafferty to the place on the top floor of the building where he belonged.

Then she hurried to Reggie's private office. She brushed against the stack of letters in her haste, rustling the ones on top slightly, but she paid no heed to that; she was on a mission. She unlocked the door with a key from her purse, went inside, and closed the door behind her.

It took her ten minutes, no more, and then Reggie's office doors opened again, and she stepped out.

Anyone watching would have seen a woman exit the office wearing hair that was black, blue, and green, black leather pants, a black leather halter top, and black lipstick. Her heavily layered, pale face looked younger than Laura Rankin's. And she appeared slightly shorter, just because of the way she was holding her posture. She was Laura Rankin as a young Goth.

She locked the office door behind her, walked quickly toward the lift, and then stopped. A letter had fallen to the floor. She knew that she must have been the one who had made that happen, and she simply could not litter and walk away. She picked it up, reached to put it back on the desk, and then stopped.

One word had caught her eye.

Bodfyn? Really?

It was in the very first line. She looked closer. Yes, that's where it was from. She read the letter, which was very short. Her eyes grew wide and she read it again. She checked her watch, and then, even though there was little time, she ran to the photocopier, made a copy, then returned the letter to its original envelope in the stack, stuffed the copy of it into her purse, and hurried on to the stairwell.

She got out to the alley without seeing anyone, or being

seen, so far as she could tell. But the fog was burning off. She began to run toward the end of the alley at Marylebone Road; she didn't slow to a fast walk until she became afraid people would notice.

She turned to her left and joined the pedestrian commuters heading toward the intersection of Marylebone Road and the two hundred block of Baker Street. She held back and waited for the light to change so that she could cross the intersection with the crowd; after that, she kept going several more yards, just past the eight-foot bronze statue of Sherlock Holmes, and then she turned left and entered the Marylebone tube station.

She was going with the flow, and that was a good thing. Whether any of the paparazzi, stationed a quarter of the way up Baker Street, had been alert enough to glance over as the light changed and notice her, she didn't know. It would have been a mistake to turn and look, so she just kept on moving.

She hurried down the stairs along with everyone else. As she reached the fork in the stairwell, where busker musicians played for tips and the crowd divided to get to one tunnel direction or the other, a blast of wind came up from a train departing to the south. She wanted the train heading north, to Charing Cross, and she could hear the roar of it coming now. Normally, she would have paused to toss in a few coins for the buskers. No time for that today. She ran down the steps and got to the platform just as the train doors opened, with the crowd pushing (in the polite

English way) and the PA system ordering everyone to mind the gap.

Now she could breathe a sigh of relief. She was on the train. Standing, to be sure, because all the seats were taken, but she was fine with that. She could sit down at Charing Cross, where she would get the overland train to Cornwall. For now, she was safe amid the crowd.

5

LONDON, THE NEXT AFTERNOON

Lord Buxton had an ear worm. A song stuck in his head. There didn't seem to be anything he could do to make it go away.

Is she really going out with him?

That was the lyric. At the suggestion of his personal secretary—a lovely girl, whose résumé included Cheltenham Ladies' College and the pages of the Victoria's Secret catalog—he was trying to get it out of his head by contemplating the Thames. After all, she had said, what was the point of having the biggest picture window in all of London if you didn't look at the river occasionally?

The remark was a bit naïve; she should have known that the point of having the biggest picture window in all

of London overlooking the Thames was just to have it—
not to waste time contemplating the river through it.

But Buxton was so desperate that he had tried it—
contemplating. And of course it didn't get rid of the ear
worm:

Is she really going out with him?

Buxton had not heard that song lyric since he was a
teenager, but he had been thinking of it for days now. He
well knew the reason why, though he was careful not to
let anyone else in on it. One doesn't reveal one's crushes;
that way lies ridicule—unless requited—even if one is the
most powerful media magnate in the world.

In any case, staring at the Thames wasn't going to help:
Laura Rankin was getting married to Reggie Heath, and
Lord Buxton could not fathom her choice. He had, in fact,
been trying to prevent this very occurrence for the past
several years—ever since meeting the woman and realizing he had to have her for himself.

His chances had looked very good at first; Heath
had just made some colossal blunder when Buxton came
on the scene. And Buxton had so much more to offer—a
motion picture company of his very own to make her
films; a media empire to celebrate them; penthouses and
châteaux everywhere in the world for the parties after;
and best of all—well, simply the fact that he was who he
was: Lord Buxton.

Not some bleedin' half-penny lawyer whose only claim
to fame was the foolishness of locating his law chambers

in the lower portion of the two hundred block of Baker Street, thereby obliging him to uphold the last vestiges of British tradition by—of all things—actually responding to letters written to Sherlock Holmes.

It was a quirky, almost humiliating requirement, at least for any respectable sort of barrister, and so Buxton had made a special point of broadcasting to the world all of Reggie Heath's most embarrassing attempts to fulfill his obligation. In recent years, as reported by Buxton's *Daily Sun*, Reggie Heath, QC, had blown up a subway tunnel in Los Angeles, set a London serial killer free and then murdered him, nearly destroyed the institution of black cabs in London, and furthered the delusions of a lunatic who believed herself to be the great-great-granddaughter of an actual Professor Moriarty.

But Buxton's most concerted efforts had not yielded the intended result. Not only had Heath won Laura Rankin back but, for some reason, she had stuck by him through all of it. And now time had run out. The wedding was today—less than an hour ago, in fact—and Lord Buxton had finally unleashed his most powerful weapon to try to stop it: the fiercest, most unscrupulous team of paparazzi in the world.

Until now, he had used a very careful touch. It wouldn't do just to swing unwelcome publicity like a sledgehammer, as Buxton's tabloid media usually did, and the devil take the consequences. He wanted to hit Reggie, not Laura. He had to wield his weapons as a surgeon would a scalpel.

Cut out the malignant competition but do no harm to the patient. Perhaps a slight scar, at most.

But today was the wedding, and he had turned them loose.

Now his personal secretary buzzed him.

"I have them online, sir," she said.

"Let's see them," said Buxton.

A very large digital screen descended now in front of the picture window. Within a few seconds, the pixels had formed, and there was Buxton's team, still on the scene at the wedding location—two men and one woman, ranging in age from twenty-six to fifty, all with expressions of deep shame and apprehension. The news could not be good.

"Well?"

"You were absolutely right, sir," said the eldest of the three paparazzi. "The cancellation was a sham. The wedding was still on. It was at the estate of Ms. Rankin's aunt in Cornwall. No one was supposed to know."

"And?"

"I used the undercover contact I made at the rehearsal. She's Reggie Heath's clerk at Baker Street Chambers, you see, and she knows practically everything. I just got her a bit tingly with wine, chatted her up, and I determined not only the location but the time and—"

"Yes, Fabio, you're a great Lothario and a tactical genius; we all get it. That's your job," said Buxton. "But what happened?"

"We have this, sir."

Fabio held up a digital thumb drive.

"Plug it in," said Buxton.

Fabio plugged the drive into his device and began his presentation, alternating between views of himself and the photos they had acquired.

"This is the back lawn of the estate. The fellow glaring at me is Spenser, the butler. Almost caught me sneaking in through the hedge, but he wasn't quite sure. This one is the wedding party beginning to assemble—that woman there, the bridesmaid with the startled look, that's Lois, the barrister's clerk I told you about, before she recognized me from the rehearsal and raised the alarm."

"Get to the point, please," said Buxton.

Now the young female paparazzo standing next to Fabio jumped in and seized the digital clicker.

"These ones are mine. I'll present them myself, if you don't mind. Now then, here's one of the groom, our Mr. Heath, standing and waiting for the bride, and—and you know, in person, he's not nearly so unattractive and silly as you said; I almost think he's rather—"

"Move on," said Buxton tersely.

"And here he is taking a swing at Fabio—which Fabio ducks, and so here you see Mr. Heath's momentum carrying him right into the wedding cake—"

"I like that one. Make a note," said Buxton.

"Of course. And now here's Fabio retreating from Mr. Heath, and now Mr. Heath again, with his hands on his face after I had to punch him to keep him from ripping Fabio's camera away. And then here's that butler fellow in a golf cart, chasing Fabio, and—"

"The bride," said Buxton, "where is Laura Rankin?"

"And here you see Laura Rankin and Reggie Heath from behind as they both run into the barn on the back lawn. And next, when the barn doors open, we have—"

"Next we have mine," said the third paparazzo, seizing the clicker, "and I risked my bloody life to get them. There—there—you see that?"

"The underside of a small plane?"

"Yes, yes—she nearly flew into me, would have cut me to shreds. I almost fell over the cliff getting out of the way!"

"She? You mean Laura?"

"Yes, the groom was in the passenger seat, and the bride was flying the bloody thing. That's how they got away. They ran into this barn at the far end of the estate, I ran after them, and then the barn doors opened and they came out in that. A Cessna 150, I think."

"What about the bloody ceremony?" said Buxton. "Did they complete the ceremony, or did they not?"

"By 'complete' it, do you mean—"

"Did they actually exchange vows?"

There was a long pause as the three paparazzi conferred. Finally, they all stuck their heads into digital view again.

"We're not sure," said Fabio.

Buxton drummed his fingers on his rosewood and ebony desk.

"Where was the plane headed?" he asked finally.

"We don't know," said Fabio. "It started out over the coast, but we think it turned when it got into the clouds."

"Well, find the bloody hell out!" said Buxton. "Don't just stand there. Go!"

Now the transmission cut off.

As the video screen retracted to its original position, Buxton went to the window and looked down at the Thames again.

Bloody hell.

Is she really going out with him?

6

CORNWALL

In the years that he had known her, Reggie had never once heard Laura mention that she knew how to fly a plane.

But she was flying one now. She in her wedding dress. He in his tux. Both of them with mud on their shoes. Laura with grass stains forever embedded in that designer dress, and deliciously moist wedding cake and frosting in her hair; Reggie with bruised knuckles on his right hand and a worse bruise under his left eye.

At the estate, as he was getting dressed, Reggie had received a note from Laura, saying that she had a backup plan—that if the paparazzi should somehow discover their wedding location and invade, she had a foolproof plan of escape for the honeymoon: They would simply abandon their reservations in the south of France, where the paparazzi would surely know to look, and go somewhere else.

She hadn't said where the somewhere else would be. Or that they would get there in a plane not much bigger than Reggie's new Range Rover. Or that she would be the pilot.

But she had done a fine job of it to this point, so far as Reggie could tell. They were still airborne, and still moving. And flying by instruments, in the dark.

But then, of course, in a plane, it is the landing that is important.

"The subject never came up," said Laura.

"What subject?"

"That I had a pilot's license."

"I didn't ask."

"You were about to."

"No, I wasn't." Then: "What do you mean, 'had'?"

"Oh, you are supposed to get retested and relicensed every so many years if you don't log enough hours, and I haven't in a while, but no matter. It's the same plane I learned in, after all, and that was only sixteen years ago, and well, of course the sky is still the sky."

"And the earth is still the earth," said Reggie. "But how do we know where it is in the dark?"

Reggie was looking down through the window on his right. They were flying above a broad cloud bank. There were stars and a waxing moon overhead, but nothing distinguishable below.

"One of these dials tells us," said Laura. "That one there. Oh, would you tap it, please? It doesn't seem to be lighting up."

Reggie tapped the dial.

"Harder," said Laura.

Reggie tapped it harder.

"Hmm," said Laura. "Well, no matter. I'm sure we'll be able to see something when we get lower."

And with that, Laura took the plane down in what felt to Reggie like a roller coaster dive.

"There, that's better," said Laura. "We're below the clouds now. Do you see anything?"

Reggie looked down.

"No. It's all black. What happened to civilization? I can't even make out the terrain—"

"Well, we're flying over the national preserve, is why. But I've flown this route once in the daylight, so I know what's below and I can give you the three-penny tour if you like. Right now we should be just over the pine—"

Reggie interrupted.

"Just once?"

"Yes. Why?"

"No reason."

"So right now we're over a patch of pine forest, and then some oaks, and after that it's mostly just moors. Out to the left is a lake, with the forest on one side and the moor on the other. Out to the right will be the village of Bodfyn, but we can't land there, so we're going just straight ahead, and any moment now, if we're low enough, we should see just one light. But I don't see it yet, do you? I suppose we'll just have to descend a little bit farther—"

"No, no, wait; let's not be hasty," said Reggie. "I think I see something. Yes, a light. Down there—well, of course—ahead and just a bit to the right."

"Ah, brilliant. There she is, just where she should be. Right, then, here we go!"

Laura took the plane down in a steady, steep slope, curving to the right—in the direction of the single, fuzzy, yellowish point of light that Reggie had spotted below.

Soon they saw the source of the light—a handheld lantern that someone was swinging back and forth—and the ground, approaching rapidly.

"Seat belt?" said Laura.

"Seriously?" said Reggie. "You think I waited until now?"

Laura cut the engine; the wheels touched; mud and grass sprayed from beneath the plane. The landing gear bounced once, but only slightly, and then the wheels touched again, this time firmly. The plane shook and wobbled, and in another moment they had come to a full stop.

"That wasn't so bad, was it?" said Laura. Now she breathed a sigh of relief herself. "Think how smooth it would have been if only we'd had an actual runway."

The lantern was no longer swinging. The person holding it—and keeping a safe distance—lifted it as high as possible now, and called out. It was a woman's voice.

"All settled, then, are we?"

"Bob's your uncle!" yelled Laura.

"I'll just get the car and be right over," yelled the woman, and then she and the lantern went away a short distance.

"My," said Laura. "That certainly got the blood up, didn't it?"

"Yes," said Reggie.

"You know what flying always makes me want to do?" said Laura. Her face was flushed, her eyes shining, and her breasts rising and falling with each adrenaline-fueled breath.

Reggie could barely see any of that, it was so dark, but he could hear it, sense it, and smell her perfume with every move.

"Can we tell the woman with the car just to go away?" he asked as they leaned in toward each other. "Perhaps if you start the propellers again?"

Too late. Headlamps shone on them now, the propellers could no longer be a deterrent, and a sleek but quirky 1970s Citroën came humming right up to the plane.

The middle-aged lantern woman jumped out of the car and ran excitedly toward them, not bothering to turn off the headlamps.

"Laura! You look wonderful!"

Laura gave Reggie an encouraging push to get out of the plane.

"Thank you, Mrs. Hatfield. So do you!"

Laura made introductions, with the three of them standing in the damp, dark meadow, framed in the lights of the car. Mrs. Hatfield, Laura said fondly, was her theater teacher from her first years of secondary school.

"And you were my very best pupil," said Mrs. Hatfield. "And my goodness, look at you now. I'm so glad you took my advice all those years ago and adopted a stage name. Nothing against Penobscott, of course, but—well, you know how very like children people in the entertainment world can be. Now, come right along, both of you. I know you don't want to dally, my little Juliet and Romeo. Mustn't be naughty out here in the open."

Laura grabbed the smaller bag, and Reggie lugged the other two. Before they reached the car, Reggie spoke in a low and puzzled voice to Laura.

"I didn't know you went to school here," he said. "I thought you grew up in Cornwall. At the castle, with your aunt."

"Oh, yes, but that was only from sixteen on. Before that—after my parents died—I went to the boarding school here. My aunt couldn't be reached, out gallivanting in the wilds of Australia somewhere, the sort of thing she was inclined to do back in the day, and my parents had already signed me up for this school, so this is where I went. For almost two years."

"Hmm. Very formative years," said Reggie.

"Why do you say that?"

"Fourteen and fifteen? Because they are."

Reggie, curious now, looked up at Laura as he pushed the bags into the boot of the car.

"Why didn't you tell me about that before?" he asked.

"Before what?"

"Well . . . before we jumped in the plane, I suppose."

"Well, I . . . it just never came up, did it?" said Laura. "Anyway, I think my plan worked rather well, don't you? Not a paparazzi . . . I mean paparazzo . . . or is it paparazza . . . anyway, none of them in sight!"

Reggie climbed into the backseat of the sedan with the one bag that wouldn't fit in the boot. Laura squeezed in next to Mrs. Hatfield in the front.

"I can't wait to catch up," said Laura as she got in. Then, leaning over to whisper, she said, "You have to tell me everything you hinted about in your letter!"

"I wrote you?" said Mrs. Hatfield. "Oh, I'm getting so forgetful. It used to be I'd forget that I hadn't written; now I'm forgetting when I do."

Mrs. Hatfield started the engine and the car spun just a little mud getting out of the field. Within a few moments, they were bumping nicely along an unpaved country road in the dark.

"It feels as though we're driving on the moon," said Laura.

"Exactly," said Mrs. Hatfield. "No one will think to

look for you here. And I'll have you both snug as two bugs in a rug in no time."

They drove on, through the nearly pitch-black darkness of an overcast night in the countryside, until finally a portion of the real moon shone through, just for a moment, as they were crossing a stonework bridge. Light glimmered off smooth-flowing water a few meters below.

"That's our little river," said Mrs. Hatfield cheerily, directing her voice to Reggie in the backseat. "It flows into a lake just a bit farther east, but you can't see it from here at night."

"I used to skip pebbles in it," said Laura.

"So I heard," said Mrs. Hatfield.

Laura and Mrs. Hatfield were reestablishing old bonds. Reggie left them to it. He sat back and settled on a mental image of the teenage Laura skimming stones, the sun glinting off her red hair and the blue water.

"We're almost there," said Mrs. Hatfield a few minutes later. Reggie looked. Indeed, some distance ahead was the blurry twinkling of one yellow streetlamp, or perhaps two.

"I hope you aren't both completely addicted to your mobile phones," said Mrs. Hatfield as the car drew closer to the town. "I'm afraid we're in a bit of a dead zone here, except when the planets or satellites or something align just right. We've got these two lovely hills to the north, and then another one, even higher, to the south. So between them, it's not great for staying in touch with the whole world minute by minute, you know, but wonderful if you want to avoid prying eyes."

Soon they were driving on the main street—the one street, as near as Reggie could tell—of Bodfyn.

All the shops—a half dozen of them—were closed and dark at this hour. Even the pub—the one pub, thought Reggie sadly—was closed now. No one was in the street.

In less than a mile, they had gone the whole length of the town. They passed the second of the two streetlamps, and then they turned left, continuing about a hundred yards down an unlit lane before coming to a stop.

"You can't tell much in the dark," she said, "and I didn't want to attract attention by leaving lights on. But when you get up in the morning—at whatever time you please, of course—you'll see that it is quite lovely, in its own way.

"The bedroom is just upstairs. It's got a lovely balcony, and on a clear day you can see all the way to—oh, I forget exactly, but it's some rock or something on top of one of our two twin hills. No jokes, please. Everything is modernized inside, and en suite, you'll be happy to know. The shower and bath were redone with pink-and-white tile less than a century ago. It's rather close quarters in there, but perhaps you won't mind too much."

She unlocked the door for them, then reached down to help carry the bags in. Laura stopped her.

"Oh, no, Mrs. Hatfield," said Laura. "Reggie can manage that. Can't you, Reggie? While Mrs. Hatfield and I just finish up here?"

Reggie stretched his legs out from riding in the cramped backseat, then carried the bags up. He put them down in the bedroom, turned on the light, and opened the balcony door. Outside, he saw a dark, overcast sky, and darker outlines of a line of trees in the distance.

At the front door, Mrs. Hatfield had finished giving houseguest instructions to Laura, and now she was about to go back to her car, but she paused.

"You know, Laura, there is one other thing—"

"Yes," said Laura. "I was wondering why you hadn't mentioned it yet."

"You were?"

"Why yes, of course. Why else do you think I'm here?"

"You're here to get away from those horrid paparazzi. Aren't you? That's what you said on the phone."

"Well, yes, that, too, but—really, we could have escaped to almost anywhere. I chose here, of course, because of your letter."

"Oh," said Mrs. Hatfield. She thought for a moment, studying the expression on Laura's face, which was one of genuine concern, and Mrs. Hatfield's own expression just grew more and more puzzled.

"You know, dear, if you still say I sent you a letter, I certainly take your word for it. But honestly, I don't remember doing so. What was it that I said in it?"

"Well, I . . . I suppose the details don't really matter, if you didn't actually send it. But you—I mean, the typed letter with your name on it—said you needed help. Quite urgently."

"Oh, surely I would remember saying that. Oh dear. I must be going just completely out of—"

"Oh, no," said Laura quickly. "It's not you; it's me, I'm sure. I mean, not that I'm going out of my mind, but—well, it's very complicated. I suppose I shouldn't have just assumed so much, given that it didn't actually have your signature . . . and also that it wasn't actually addressed to me."

"Laura, dear, are you feeling all right? You know, a wedding can be a very stressful thing, and perhaps—"

Laura laughed, partly out of embarrassment, but mostly out of relief.

"I am fine, Mrs. Hatfield. Truly. I am just so glad that you are, too, and that you don't actually need my help, I mean—not that I wouldn't do just anything for you—"

"Well, of course you would. I know that, Laura, dear. Now, I want you to go inside and get yourself a nice glass of wine, and then go right upstairs, and you and Reggie just—well, whatever."

"Thank you. Good night, Mrs. Hatfield."

"Good night, dear."

Mrs. Hatfield began to walk away to her car again, but once more she stopped and turned around.

"Was there something else?" asked Laura.

Mrs. Hatfield laughed, just a bit self-consciously.

"You know, I wasn't going to mention it at all, but—"

"Yes?"

"Since you are here, I thought you might like to know that we are about to open a new theater in Bodfyn."

"Oh, how wonderful!"

"Yes, isn't it? I think every community needs its own stage. And also, with your old boarding school closed, there is no place at all for young people to learn their craft here anymore."

"Yes, I did hear about that. It's a shame."

"But now we've created the Bodfyn Players, and opening night for our very first production is this coming weekend!"

"Brilliant!"

"Yes, and not only that, but the proceeds will go to a fund dedicated to getting the school reopened."

"Well, that's a good cause, I suppose," said Laura. "I mean, most certainly, if you really can manage it."

"Yes, but you know, we have encountered just the tiniest little glitch—one of our actresses has . . . well, I don't want to talk about sad things on your first night here, but, well, there was a bit of a . . . hiking accident, and so we lost her."

"Oh. I'm so sorry."

"Yes. Now, it's not a very complicated role—well, I mean for the right person—and I could find someone to fill in, I'm sure, but it would be such a challenge for her to learn all the lines in time that—that what's really needed is someone with real experience and stage presence, someone so professional that she could just step in for the weekend and—well, you know—it would only be for the Saturday premiere and then the Sunday matinee. We'll have someone else in place for the next weekend after."

Laura, standing in the doorway and looking at Mrs. Hatfield's imploring expression, suddenly realized what was being asked.

"Oh," she said.

"We wouldn't tell anyone that it is you, of course. We would preserve your secret identity, and not announce you as a special guest star or anything like that. You would only be a more or less anonymous stand-in who is astonishingly good at it!"

Mrs. Hatfield stopped now, realizing that her enthusiasm had gotten the better of her, and that Laura had not yet said a word in response.

"But I'm so very sorry," said the woman. "I shouldn't have mentioned anything about it at all, and I wasn't going to, but—"

"Mrs. Hatfield," said Laura emphatically, "I would be absolutely delighted to help out in any way I can."

On the balcony, Reggie looked down at this scene and wondered why Laura and Mrs. Hatfield were taking so long. He could see that they were still chatting, but how could they have so much to talk about? And even if they did, what part of "We're on our honeymoon" did Mrs. Hatfield not understand?

Then there was the fact that—though he supposed it was probably just his own imagination, given what they'd been through that day, the unusual surroundings, the late hour, and everything else, including the fact that he hadn't been able to get a pint—somehow the body postures of Laura and her onetime theater mentor seemed, well, surprisingly tense and businesslike.

Finally, Laura nodded, agreeably, so far as Reggie could tell. She gave Mrs. Hatfield a quick hug, and as Mrs. Hatfield finally got in her car, Laura picked up the remaining small bag and came inside. Moments later, she was upstairs.

"What was all that about?" asked Reggie.

"All what?"

"Down below," said Reggie, indicating the front porch.

Laura smiled.

"Seriously?" she said. "It's the first night of our honeymoon—and that's the down below you're thinking about?"

7

I have a surprise for you," said Laura the next morning. She was stepping out of the shower, and it was indeed close quarters. Reggie had a big white towel ready for her, so fluffy that there was barely room to turn around.

"I have a surprise for you, too," he said.

"Oh. So you do! But let's go into the village and I'll show you mine first. Be a dear and save yours for later. Though I am duly impressed."

Some thirty minutes later, Laura having changed her mind about priorities in dealing with surprises, they walked down the little lane and onto the main street of the village.

The sky had cleared, and as Mrs. Hatfield had promised, the town in daylight was pleasant. The street was paved with gray bricks. They were flanked on both sides by cottages—some of them residences, others converted to small-business use—of white plaster, with brown shingled roofs and brightly flowering front gardens. They passed the town's one auto garage, a hairdresser's, a tearoom.

Laura was in disguise again—now more toward local punk rocker than Goth—but as they started out, Reggie wondered if it would be enough.

"You know," he said, "it won't do us much good to have come here if someone recognizes you and turns us in to the paparazzi. There's a reward out. And if they trap us in this isolated place, we'll have the devil of a time getting away. Are you sure you won't be recognized?"

"Oh, I don't think so. Not with my blue hair and lip ring. Do you like it? Don't answer yet. Wait till later."

"It might be enough to fool the casual observer. But what if we run into some of your old school chums?"

"Oh no, I'm sure not. They will all have long since moved on. That was the whole point of the little boarding school. Get in, get out, move on. I believe it's inscribed in Latin above the main door. Some of the crasser boys used to joke that's how they wanted their dating lives to be. Anyway, this is one of those little places that people come from—but tend not to go to if they can help it."

"Yet here we are," said Reggie.

"Yes, but at least it's much cheerier in daylight, don't you think?"

Laura pointed out the flowers everywhere, and not just the geraniums in the windows and roses in the gardens but also the white-and-yellow daisies and purple lythrums that seemed to be growing nearly everywhere.

"Yes," said Reggie, with a wave out beyond the town. "And the clumps of sheep and bunches of cows and murders of crows are all quite pastoral as well, in both scent and sound."

"Now, don't be a city grump," said Laura. "I know you don't like crows, ever since that incident in the Cotswolds, but this is nothing like that. And it's wool that comes in clumps, by the way, not the sheep themselves. Oh, look, we're here!"

They were standing in front of an eighteenth-century church. Or, at least, that's what it certainly had been. The blocks were gray-white granite, with color variations that had developed over centuries. Deep green leaves of ivy made inroads, contrasting brightly with the rock.

Visible behind the roof of the church were the tops of a stand of Scots pines, and to one side was a row of Douglas firs, imported and planted in the past century or so. A path of smooth garden pavers led to the front steps, and above the entrance was a banner that proclaimed the structure's current purpose: BODFYN THEATRE COMPANY—PREMIERE!

Just as Reggie was digesting that, the heavy front doors opened—and out came Mrs. Hatfield:

"Ah! There you are!"

She hurried across the pavers to meet Laura halfway.

"I'm so sorry to be late, Mrs. Hatfield. Reggie and I just—"

"Oh, no need to explain, my dear," said Mrs. Hatfield coyly. She added in mock secrecy to Laura, "But you can tell me all about it later, if you like!"

Mrs. Hatfield walked them both to the entrance. She put a hand on Reggie's shoulder. "Are you coming in with us? Or would you just prefer directions to our pub, the Wayward Pony, as all the other husbands seem to prefer during our rehearsals? When the weather's right, it has the most delightful view of the moor. The only spot in town that does, really. It's quite the little gathering place. There's only the one, everyone goes there, and it is—that way."

She pointed down the street toward the opposite end of the village.

Laura, with just the tiniest bit of apprehension, said, "Oh, I'm sure Reggie would like to see the theater first! Wouldn't you?"

"Ah . . . give us just a moment?" said Reggie.

"Of course, my dears," said Mrs. Hatfield.

She went inside, shut the entrance doors halfway, and left them just partly alone for a moment.

"Now, don't be upset," said Laura quickly. "I only found out myself last night, when we arrived, and—and, well, you certainly wouldn't have wanted me to say anything about it at that time, would you? Please say you wouldn't."

"This . . . this is the surprise?"

"Well . . . yes. Mrs. Hatfield just needs a little help with their new theater company."

"How about a modest financial donation? I'll be happy to write a check."

"Well, no, that's not the sort of help she requested."

"Painting sets for an afternoon?"

"No, I'm afraid that would not do it."

"Advising their board of directors about play selections for the coming season?"

"No, I'm afraid it's too late for that."

There was a long pause.

"Now, Reggie, don't give me that look, and don't be obtuse. You know perfectly well what an established actress means when she says her hometown theater company has asked for her help."

"How long?"

"Just a few days of rehearsal and then one weekend of performances. They're already in full dress; they open on Saturday. I know the play well, so all I really need to do is learn their blocking. Now, don't sulk. I wouldn't be doing it if it weren't such an emergency for them."

"I . . . well, just what sort of bloody emergency is it, exactly?"

"Now, darling, you won't go into barrister mode on me, will you? I'm substituting for the local actress, who apparently had some sort of small accident. They wouldn't be asking me otherwise."

"What happened? Did someone wish her to 'break a leg' and she did?"

"Mrs. Hatfield didn't say, but I doubt it was anything too terrible. People have their day jobs and their day lives in these amateur productions, you know, and sometimes life just intrudes."

They both looked up now as a group of large blackbirds flew disturbingly close overhead and took roost in the nearby pines.

Then the theater doors opened and Mrs. Hatfield appeared.

"Ready, dears? Oh, did I tell you the theme of our premiere? It's 'Shakespeare as He Should Have Been.'"

"What was that?" asked Laura. "I couldn't hear, those crows made such a racket."

Mrs. Hatfield explained patiently.

"We recognize that the Bard was a person of his time, and therefore cannot be held to the more developed sensibilities of today. Still, if our young people are going to continue to study Shakespeare, we need to point out the microaggressions in his plays when they are read, with warning notes in the margins and such, and when they are performed, we must perform them with those flaws removed, through clever casting choices and edits in dialogue and plot where necessary."

"Seriously?" said Reggie.

Laura pulled him aside, a couple of steps away from Mrs. Hatfield, and then, after a quick glance back, a couple more steps to be sure.

"Yes, I know," said Laura very quietly. "It's a bit silly, but she's a very nice woman, and she means well. Please try not to be a lawyer for a bit, and play nice, won't you?"

Reggie gave it a moment's thought, then nodded.

"I can mind my p's and q's if you can," he said with a slight smile.

"Is there something wrong?" asked Mrs. Hatfield.

"No," said Reggie, still smiling. "But you are preaching to the wrong congregation if your theme is to put a muzzle on Laura."

"Reggie, don't be silly," said Laura quickly. Then she turned to Mrs. Hatfield. "It's all fine. But am I to be one of those clever casting choices?"

"Only a bit," said the woman. "You look too young for the role by a decade or so, but then so did Melanie, and that can be handled with makeup. You will be Lady—" Mrs. Hatfield stopped herself. "My, I almost said it out loud. Well, we're not quite inside the theater yet, so it's all right. But we are on the doorstep, so I suppose I'd better just whisper it to you."

Mrs. Hatfield did so, quite inaudibly, from Reggie's perspective.

"Oh," said Laura with some surprise. "When you said a small role, I thought—"

"Oh, it is; I mean mostly—we've cut out most of the longer parts. Don't worry, you'll be fine; I know your ability to play anyone, no matter how contrary to natural character. Well. Shall we go in?"

They entered the former church. It had smooth hardwood benches on either side, with seating for perhaps two hundred.

They began to walk down the center aisle toward the stage.

"Such an intimate setting for Shakespeare," said Laura. "I'll bet you can hear a whisper from the farthest row!"

"No doubt," said Reggie. "By the way, which bit of Shakespeare is it?"

"It's the Scottish play," said Mrs. Hatfield.

"Yes, but which one?"

"The Scottish play."

"Oh. Must have been one of his lesser works, if no one even remembers the name."

Mrs. Hatfield walked up close to Laura and whispered again. "Has your husband never even been to the theater?"

"I heard that," said Reggie.

"Of course he has," said Laura. "It's how we met. He saw me in *Chicago*. He's just been too busy to go again since. Either that or he's already got what he wanted."

"Ah. That explains why he doesn't know we never say the name of this play once inside the theater."

"Why not?" asked Reggie. "I don't recall any Shakespeare titles that are embarrassing to say. Except *Titus Andronicus*, and that's only if you mispronounce it."

"The druid witches put a curse on this one centuries ago. If you say the word inside the theater, they have to kill you. Or other bad things can happen."

"Now, Mrs. Hatfield, stop trying to scare my new husband."

"Oh, the one with the witches," said Reggie. "Now I get it. But the name of the play is the same as the name of the main character of the play, is it not?"

"Yes, that's correct," said Mrs. Hatfield.

"So what if someone says the name of the main character inside the theater? I'm sure that must happen in the course of the play. Is the curse smart enough to recognize the context in which the word is being used?"

Mrs. Hatfield hesitated, and Laura saw her discomfort.

"Now, Reggie . . ." said Laura.

"The curse does not apply if you say it as a character within the play and on the stage, in either rehearsal or performance," said Mrs. Hatfield. "Only outside of it. I'm almost certain."

"Ah, I suppose that's the nature of really effective curses," said Reggie. "Very particular and completely arbitrary at the same time. So if the name of the play cannot be spoken, what about other forms of communication? Would one be allowed to draw a picture?"

"Reggie, you promised. We're not in the Old Bailey."

"Hmm," said Mrs. Hatfield. "I think probably not. I mean, not of the title character anyway."

"Oh, that can't be right," said Laura. "I'm sure I've seen depictions of Laurence Olivier playing the role of—well, you know—and the name of it plastered right there on the poster with him!"

"Yes," said Mrs. Hatfield. "And look what happened to him!"

Laura looked puzzled at first, but now Reggie had caught on, and he nodded.

"He died," said Reggie.

"Oh, don't mind him," said Laura to Mrs. Hatfield. "He's just doing what he's been trained to do. Reggie, stop it."

"Sorry."

Now they had reached the foot of the stage, and Laura stopped.

"Oh, is it not quite ready yet?"

Mrs. Hatfield admitted that it was not, and that one cannot trod the boards when not all the boards are there.

"We're just finishing a bit of structural renovation. We had a slight delay with the archaeological preservation committee, but we're back on track now. Don't worry, my dear," she said to Laura. "You won't be putting your foot through open space on opening night. Now, let's just go backstage, and I'll introduce everyone."

They avoided the stage itself, and walked around a side aisle to a single room behind it that served as the greenroom—and the makeup room, and the dressing area, and the prop storage.

Most of the actors were there, all of them in some state of undress, getting ready to go onstage for the next rehearsal.

Reggie tried to remember whether there were any Shakespearean plays that typically required female nudity, of the sort that would give the director an excuse to try to demand that the actress demonstrate her comfort in being nude onstage by first disrobing for the director in private.

"Will this be a fully clothed version of the Scottish play?" he asked.

"What?" said the director.

"Oh, don't mind Reggie," said Laura to the director. "He's just worried that you'll try to insist on the leads doing a bit of pagan nudity, like they did with the witches a while back in Central Park."

The director looked crestfallen, and he said to Laura with apparent sincerity, "You would . . . find that objectionable?"

"I certainly would, in this weather."

"As would I on her behalf," said Reggie. "In any weather."

Laura nudged the director.

"We're still on honeymoon," she said. "And you test my husband at your peril."

The director, a smallish, balding man in his late fifties, nodded and changed the subject. He began talking about how once he had almost been cast as the understudy to a fellow who had almost been cast as Richard III some ten years earlier, when Laura had been on the London stage for the very first time, playing the character of the young Elizabeth.

What karma, the man kept saying, that fate had brought them together for Shakespeare again—and with him as her director!

Of course, said the man, with a rather wry smile, their careers had gone rather differently since that time.

"So," said Reggie, trying to be conversational, "what do you do in real life now?"

Laura and Mrs. Hatfield both gasped. Everyone else backstage went immediately silent. Some people turned to look, others were afraid to, and Reggie sensed fairly quickly that he had committed yet another faux pas.

The former candidate to almost be the understudy for Richard in *Richard III*, stared at Reggie with a look of deep offense and distress.

"The theater," he said, "is my life!"

And then he rushed out of the room.

"Oh dear," said Mrs. Hatfield. "I'd better try to calm him down. Laura, perhaps if you come along, too—"

"Certainly," said Laura. She whispered to Reggie that he should try not to break anything, and then she hurried after Mrs. Hatfield to help salvage the director.

Reggie found himself on his own now backstage. He looked around for safe harbor.

There was a gray-haired prop mistress, who was busy spraying silver paint on some sort of fake sword; the leading man, Reggie's age or perhaps a few years older, sitting in front of the makeup mirror; and a young woman wearing a putty nose, a plastic wart, dark eye shadow, and not very much else, who seemed to be helping the leading man get his hair right in some way.

Reggie wondered whom he might safely talk to. The prop woman seemed the best choice, even though Laura had specifically told him not to break anything. But perhaps if he just spoke clearly and remained very still—"

"Making a fake sword, then?" said Reggie.

Immediately it occurred to him that if the prop mistress was anywhere near as sensitive as the director, he probably shouldn't have used the word *fake*.

But, fortunately, she did not seem to take offense.

"Nothing fake about it," said the woman, now ready to inspect her work. She raised the sword up at a ninety-degree angle with both hands and gave a slight smile. "Just spraying over the rust."

"Ah," said Reggie. He took a step back. "Good to know."

Now the young woman wearing witch's makeup, who to this point had seen Reggie only in the mirror's reflection, stepped back from doing the leading man's hair and gave Reggie a look in person. A very long look.

"Hullo," she said.

"Hello," said Reggie.

"You're very tall," she said. "Much more suited for this play than some of the other men in the cast."

She stepped up closer to him.

It must be the wedding ring, thought Reggie. He took a half step back, putting himself right up against the wall.

"And you have a wonderful speaking voice. What role do you play?"

"Husband," said Reggie.

The young woman's eyes glimmered, and she retreated not an inch.

Then Laura returned.

"Careful, dear," said Laura, with just the slightest glance, as she sat down to do her own makeup. "My husband doesn't fully understand about theater dressing rooms, and all sexes in their knickers or less, pretending that they don't notice. You'll make him blush, or something."

"Oh, you're married to each *other*? I see. How wonderful for you!"

"Yes. So he's not accustomed to strange women's breasts in his face anymore. If you keep doing what you're doing, he'll harken back to the day and think he's supposed to throw money on the bar for you."

The young woman's smile froze, and she turned away to puzzle over whether Laura had said something catty.

"Speaking of which," said Reggie quickly, "do you suppose the pub is open now?"

"Excellent idea," said Laura. "Why don't you just go on ahead? I'll catch up with you."

"Yes, and it won't be too long," said Mrs. Hatfield. "We'll just do a quick run-through."

"Brilliant," said Reggie, happily turning to go. "I'd be glad to stay and watch you all rehearse, of course, if I hadn't already seen *Macbeth*."

Everyone gasped. Someone's hairbrush clunked to the floor. The taste of superstitious terror was palpable.

"Oh dear," said Mrs. Hatfield.

"What?" said Reggie.

"He said it!" cried one of the other three young witches, still struggling to pull her costume on over her panty hose. "He said *Mac*—well, you know!"

"Please," said Reggie. "Surely, all of you don't really believe such—"

"Oh, the curse is real enough all right," said the leading man as he scrutinized the black-and-white strands in his beard. "Melanie said it, and look what happened to her!"

"Something happened?" said Reggie. "The woman in the role before Laura didn't simply quit?"

"Oh, we don't need to go there right now, do we?" said Mrs. Hatfield.

"Now everyone just keep calm," said Laura. "No need to panic. Reggie will just go outside and do the routine, and then everything will be fine. Won't you, Reggie?"

"Certainly. What's the routine?" asked Reggie.

Laura looked to Mrs. Hatfield.

"I don't think we can say that out loud inside the theater, either," said Mrs. Hatfield. "Especially the words he has to say to make the curse go away."

"Well, you can whisper it to me first, and then I'll whisper in Reggie's ear. He'll like that anyway."

"All right, then," said Mrs. Hatfield. "Here is what he must do."

Mrs. Hatfield whispered into Laura's ear.

"Oh," said Laura, listening intently. "Oh. Yes, I see. Oh my. You know, I think I made Reggie do something very like that early this morning."

"I heard that," said Reggie.

"Well, remember it, then, and next time I won't need to do so much prompting."

"Now, the words he must say are these," said Mrs. Hatfield, continuing, and she whispered some more.

"Ah," said Laura. "Yes, yes, not a problem. I've heard him say those very words occasionally, though not in that order, and under quite different circumstances."

Now Laura turned and whispered it all to Reggie.

"If you insist," said Reggie when she was done,

"although I'd find it much easier to do after I've had my pints than before."

"Off you go. I'll catch up with you, just as soon as we're all done learning our places here."

Reggie pulled his mac close and nearly ran from the room.

Laura turned her attention to getting ready to go onstage. She glanced in the mirror.

The leading actor, seated in the prestige position at the makeup table, did not look over at her directly, but he did look at her in the mirror.

"You know," he said, "with you stepping in on such short notice, we'll hardly have enough rehearsal time to get to know each other before opening—so perhaps you'd like to step down to the pub with me later tonight? I mean, so that we can establish the proper chemistry for our stage interaction, as it were?"

Laura thought that she had been flashing her new diamond ring sufficiently that everyone in the little room should have noticed. Perhaps the gentleman had been so absorbed with himself in the mirror that he didn't see it. Or perhaps he simply didn't care.

"No," said Laura in a tone that made the rejection very clear. "I do acting. I don't do chemistry."

The leading man seemed unfazed.

"Your predecessor and I got to know each other quite well," he said. "We do play husband and wife, you know."

Laura had now had quite enough, but she refrained from slapping the man; partly because he might have enjoyed it, but mainly because she was distracted—she wasn't sure why—by the way he had said "predecessor."

8

In the pub a few hours later, Charlie, the bartender, poured Reggie's third pint and said, "You're staying at Mrs. Hatfield's holiday rental, aren't you?"

Reggie gave the bartender a questioning look. The man was in his mid-thirties, and gregarious in a chip-on-the-shoulder sort of way that Reggie associated with former school athletes trying to recapture their glory days.

"Saw you drive in," the bartender continued. "I was just then locking up. I looked down the street, and I saw Mrs. Hatfield with you and your lovely lady companion."

"That would be my wife," said Reggie.

"So you and the missus, then? On holiday, are you? We don't get many of those around here, you know."

"Holidays?"

"Tooo-rists," said the man, rather emphatically wiping down the bar in front of Reggie with a white cloth.

Reggie said nothing in response to that. Acknowledging their honeymoon in the pub would attract too much attention, and next thing, the paparazzi would be circling.

So Reggie just shrugged.

The bartender gave him a glare to indicate the insufficiency of that response, and then went away.

The pub was not crowded at the moment. There were two men discussing something vigorously at the other end of the bar, and some people occupying the two back booths. Reggie contentedly drank his beer alone. When his glass was nearly empty, he began to look around, and didn't see the bartender.

But after a moment, the barmaid came over.

"Foster's?" said Reggie.

She picked up his empty glass but didn't go to refill it yet.

"Can I ask you something?" she said, leaning in earnestly.

"Yes."

"Is it true what they say about community theater?"

"I'm not sure," said Reggie. "What do they say?"

"I mean, about the leading men and the leading ladies?"

"Again, I'm still not quite sure—"

"That they only do it so that they can meet and flirt and then—well, do it?"

"Say again?"

"I mean, there's no money in it at all, and no one's

going to get noticed and make a career from a little village like this, so that means he's only in it for the shag, right?"

"And you are referring to—"

"The leading man, of course. My boyfriend. Opposite your lady. In the bedchamber scenes."

The barmaid gave Reggie a nudging, knowing look.

"Ah . . . well, fortunately this play is not exactly a romance."

"What's romance got to do with it?"

Reggie pondered that, and the barmaid continued.

"Don't pretend you aren't worried, too. I know how women are about my Joey. She'll make a move on him, she will. I mean, let's be honest—you're a decent-enough fellow in your own right, I'm sure, but he's—well, he's Joey, and other girls just can't help themselves. And don't get me wrong; he's true to me—in his own way, I keep him happy, I do—but he's got his weaknesses, just like any other man. All that emotional pretending and dressing and undressing going on backstage—she's not as pretty as me, true, but she's nearer at hand for the next few nights, so there's good reason for concern. So, what do you think?"

"I . . . I've forgotten what your question was," said Reggie.

"My question is, if you were any kind of a man, you'd do something about it before they get all cozy for the weekend, if you want my opinion."

Reggie thought better of pointing out that this wasn't

actually a question. And he wanted to avoid further details of her opinion.

"Can I have another Foster's?" he said instead.

The barmaid gave Reggie a look of incredulous disappointment, and she took his empty away.

Reggie wondered whether he would actually be able to get another beer, and began to look around for some other pub staff to offend.

He was interrupted from this pursuit when a boisterous commotion erupted outside, and the front door flew open.

It was the entire bloody cast from the theater.

They were led in by Mrs. Hatfield. She was followed by the director, who seemed fully recovered from his earlier career angst. Then a handful of other actors, including both an older witch and a younger one, but not including the leading man.

And then, finally, Laura. A bit sheepishly.

She gave an obligatory laugh in response to something that one of the other cast members said, and then she went directly up to Reggie and sat next to him at the bar.

"I'm sorry," she said. "I tried to just sneak out, but there is only the one pub, and you know this is what theater people tend to do after dress rehearsal."

The bartender was back, at the other end of the bar, but he looked in their direction when Laura spoke. He finished what he was pouring and then came right over.

"What will the lady have?"

"Same as his," said Laura.

The bartender nodded, looked carefully at both of them for no obvious reason—although Reggie thought he might have been staring at Laura's lip ring—and then he went away.

After he did, Reggie said, "I had just hoped not to share you quite so much on our honeymoon."

"I know," said Laura, and she was silent for a moment before adding, "But, Reggie, if I don't do this, then we have no cover. We need the excuse for being here. They don't get many tourists."

"I've heard that."

"Word would get around, and next thing you know, we'd have paparazzi just everywhere again, like in London, when you threw one off the balcony and got arrested."

Laura said that in a whisper, because now the bartender was back with their pints.

"Anything else?" he asked.

"No," said Reggie.

The bartender seemed willing to hover near them even so, wiping things down that he had already wiped, leaving the barmaid on her own to deal with both the theater celebrants and the locals.

At the opposite end of the bar, a man with Einsteinish gray hair set his empty glass impatiently on the bar. He glared toward their end of the bar, wanting his refill, and though he wasn't banging his glass on the counter yet, he was sliding it around in a circular motion that seemed to indicate his patience was wearing thin.

Laura noticed, and she looked at the bartender and nodded in the man's direction.

The bartender grimaced and said, "That man is the bane of my existence. I wish he'd just leave, like the others." Then the bartender went to do his job.

Reggie looked at Laura for a moment, studying her blue hair and lip ring, and said, "Do you still think it's enough? Your disguise?"

"Oh yes," said Laura. "Between the way they make me up for the cinema and the way I've done myself up now, and the different contexts—oh yes, I don't think anyone will place me as Laura Rankin, famous actress." She laughed. "I mean, if anyone really does think of me that way, which I find truly amazing."

"Me, too," said Reggie. "But what I meant was, what if there is still someone in town who knew you back in the day? Will they know you now? Will you know them?"

Laura shook her head.

"No. I was only here for a year and a half, and the only impression I made on anyone was Mrs. Hatfield. Even she wouldn't have known it was me if we hadn't stayed in touch. If you saw my yearbook photo, you'd understand."

"I would very much like to see your yearbook photo," said Reggie.

Now Laura—with both her pint and Reggie's new one just barely begun—looked around at the noise and festivity in the bar, with all her newly found theater acquaintances laughing and roaring, and she said in Reggie's ear, loudly enough to be heard, "You know what?"

"What?"

"I think I've paid my postrehearsal dues for the evening. Why don't you and I just—"

"I agree," said Reggie. "Let's."

Reggie stood and finished his pint in one draft, and Laura began to do the same to hers, but it was taking her two drafts, and that was just one too many for an effective escape.

"Oh, you two lovebirds aren't leaving already, are you? Oh, please don't, not just yet!"

It was Mrs. Hatfield. She was slightly and cheerily drunk.

"You must at least come see the view from the back deck; it's amazing! Come along, right this way!"

Reggie was about to object, but Mrs. Hatfield already had a tipsy hand on Laura's elbow, guiding her along toward the back of the pub.

Reggie followed, going through the back door and out onto a wooden deck with outdoor tables, none of them currently in use. It was some ten feet above the slope behind the pub. The land leveled off a few yards farther out, then gradually climbed again toward the two hills in the distance.

An inebriated local, mid-fifties, thinning on top, and clearly someone who had enjoyed his pints all his life, thinking, apparently, that the invitation was meant for him as well, came happily along with them.

"There," said Mrs. Hatfield, making a sweeping gesture, when they got outside. "This is the only spot in town from which you can look between the hills and see the Bodfyn Moor valley. Isn't it lovely!"

"I'd agree with you," said Reggie, "but at the moment I don't see much of anything."

"Well, that's just the fog and all. You're used to the big city views of London, of course. This view is completely pastoral. If you come back when it's clear, you'll see what I mean. If you look to the right, you'll see a hill, and probably a sheep or three. If you look to the left, you'll see another hill, and more sheep, and if you are very lucky, perhaps even some wild ponies. But if you look right between the two hills, and especially if you put a coin in our little tourist telescope, you can see all the way to the main— Oh, what is the name? I always think of them as just a bunch of rocks. Ah, I remember—cairns. You can see all the way to the beginning of the cairn field. And then from there, if you keep hiking to your left, you can go all the way to the lake and to the most complete cairn circle of the Bodfyn Moor!"

The local with the thinning hair tried to help, stepping to the railing with a sweeping gesture of his own, and spilling only a little of his beer.

Laura stepped adroitly out of the way.

"It's right out there, beyond the rise!" he said, pointing.

"And just a clutter of stones, not a proper circle at all. So a cairn clutter is what I'd call it. Other than that, all you see is just meadow and sheep. Or sheep and meadow, as you prefer."

"Yes, as I said, pastoral," said Mrs. Hatfield.

"And the occasional druid, back in the day."

"Oh, that's just an old wives' tale," said Mrs. Hatfield.

"Very true," said the local. "It was my old wife that told me, and her mum that told her, and so on, back as far you like. Doesn't mean it ain't so. They used to pick out a likely sheep and coax it down the valley behind those two hills for the sacrifice of the spring equinox!"

"If you say so, Mr. Hennessey," said Mrs. Hatfield. "I won't argue with you."

"I will," said an educated voice behind them.

It was the impatient man with the gray hair, in a friendlier mood now that he had his pint.

"There are a couple of tallish stones out there, dragged to the location somehow by humankind a few millennia ago. But the question of what, if anything, was ever sacrificed there is very much in dispute."

"Scoff all you want," said Hennessey, the local. "I myself have seen sheep bones on the moor! So there you have it!"

He sloshed with his glass again, and once more Laura dodged successfully.

"Please be more careful, Mr. Hennessey," said Mrs. Hatfield. And then she added, as an aside to Laura, "Pay him no mind. There are sheep bones in this countryside just everywhere; it's what you get when you have sheep!"

"Oh, I know that," said Laura. "It's Reggie you need to reassure. He's been a city boy all his life."

Now the gray-haired local with the educated voice, well into his cups himself, began to get a bit beer-pensive.

"There was a lot to commend it, you know," he said almost wistfully. "Not like the more recent centuries, with all this nonsense about the individual's personal relationship with the power of the universe and people allowed to say just anything they want about it. Those were difficult times back then, and the druids weren't just the spiritual leaders; they were the organizers and lawgivers of the society, as well. Any religion must be right for its times. And those were very troubled times."

"I've known troubled times myself," said Hennessey, clearly the drunker of the two informative locals. "You know what I do about them?"

"Yes, we certainly do, Mr. Hennessey," said Mrs. Hatfield. "And you know what? I'm going to buy you another—because we still must do our toasts!"

With that, Mrs. Hatfield ushered Laura and Reggie back into the pub; she grabbed a bottle of champagne from the bar along the way, managed to fill her own glass, and began filling those of anyone she could reach.

"Everyone! Let us all now drink to our new Lady Macbeth, stepping in on such terribly short notice, my dear, dear friend, Lau—"

She stopped, finally comprehending the alarmed look on Laura's face, and made the best adjustment she could.

"Lau—aaaady Macbeth!"

Mrs. Hatfield put her glass to her lips, and so did everyone else, paying no attention to her apparent botching of the details of the toast.

She had barely swallowed that one before she raised her glass for another.

"And!" She paused for a moment as the not-drunk part of her mind tried to focus. "Everyone settle down, please, just for one minute. I'm serious. Let us raise a glass to dear Melanie, poor girl."

Everyone in the pub raised their glasses. A portly middle-aged couple standing near Laura, apparently confused by the proceedings, made sure they clinked her glass, and Mrs. Hatfield called out the toast: "To Melanie!"

Reggie and Laura drank the toast and again prepared to leave. The barmaid came over to get their glasses, and as Reggie got out his wallet, he asked, "So, what is it that happened to Melanie?"

The barmaid paused.

"When you say 'happened,' do you mean—"

"He means, how was she hurt?" said Laura.

"Oh, you mean how did she die?"

"She died?" said Laura.

"It was a hiking accident."

"What sort of hiking accident?" asked Reggie, but the barmaid didn't seem to hear.

"No, no, put your money away," she said. "It's been paid for. G'night, luvs."

Reggie would have asked who it was that had paid, but the barmaid ran off before he could.

Now he and Laura were outside. The flagstones on the path were damp, the street quiet, and the air brisk. Not an unpleasant night.

"So it's a secret, then?" said Reggie as they walked back to the house.

"What is? I'm sure it was Mrs. Hatfield who picked up the tab."

"I mean the accident that happened to Melanie."

"Why on earth would it be a secret?" said Laura.

"I don't know. But no one has said, have they?"

"No, but . . . as I said, sometimes life intrudes."

"Or death does."

"Well, yes. I'm sure it was something quite ordinary, though, don't you?" said Laura.

That question—coming from Laura—struck Reggie as odd. After all, she was the theater expert. Why was she asking him?

"Don't you?" he said.

"Well, if she'd been murdered or abducted by aliens or something, I suppose Mrs. Hatfield would likely have canceled the performance," said Laura, still sounding a bit odd to Reggie. "Although it's a fund-raiser, so—"

"And there's that 'show must go on' thing," said Reggie.

"Yes."

A moment later as they walked, Laura suddenly looked down and said, "Why is there no mud on your shoes?"

Reggie looked down.

"Should there be?"

"There should be if you performed the ritual properly, as we all told you to do."

"Oh," said Reggie.

"Tsk," said Laura, and she shook her head.

"Perhaps I cleaned them after?"

"Liar. You didn't do it at all, did you?"

Reggie kept silent.

Laura laughed. "Well. We are certainly in it now, then, aren't we?"

Then she sighed and said, "Can we take a drive in the country tomorrow? Perhaps a picnic lunch? I don't have to be back for the final rehearsal until five."

"That's the best idea I've heard since we got here," said Reggie.

"Oh, you think so, do you? We'll see what you say in the morning. Tonight I've a few other ideas of my own."

9

They drove in a vintage MGB two-seater, rented from the local garage. It was a butterscotch convertible, and because the sky was clear, they had the top down, despite the early-spring chill.

"What are you looking at?" asked Reggie.

"Those big white rocks in the field," said Laura.

"Ah. More cairns. Now if you had said, 'Oh, I know what to do for our honeymoon! Let's go to Stonehenge!' that would have been something."

Laura laughed.

"I don't think they're quite that significant. Anyway, my experience of them is a little more personal. A boy tried to persuade me to lose my virginity out there once."

"What? Do you mean to say that you went out there and almost—"

"I thought I told you. This is where I went to school!"

"Well, yes, but I thought you just meant things like Latin and geometry."

"Is that all you learned in school?"

"Pretty much. I did take an academic course in physiology, but no one would let me try any practical applications until university."

"Oh. Sorry."

"Now about that boy and the virginity thing—"

"Oh, that only happened once. It was just before I left Bodfyn and went to live with my aunt. I was almost sixteen."

"Once is as many times as that can happen, isn't it?"

"I've heard that. Anyway, our history professor came along and shooed us off."

"In the nick of time?"

Laura laughed.

"Oh, I would say there were quite a few nicks left. He only got a little fresh. Anyway, when I said no, he tried to impress me by doing a carving in one of the rocks—you know, my initials, a heart, his initials—but he didn't get very far before Mr. Turner came along."

"Hmm," said Reggie. "Speaking of fresh, I can do that, to whatever degree suits you."

She laughed again.

"Why do you suppose I brought a picnic blanket? But let's just drive on a bit, shall we? It's starting to cloud up, and I think—oh, wait, what's that?"

They had just come over a small rise.

To their left in the valley below were three wide green pastures, separated by hedgerows.

To their right, a narrow road diverged from the one they were on. It curved across a broad meadow, and behind a stand of tall silver birches, to the only structure visible in the valley.

"Turn there!" said Laura.

"Why?"

"I'll show you. Just turn!"

Reggie did. The MGB took the curve nimbly, and in a moment they were whirring down the road, beneath the light canopy of the silver beeches.

They pulled to a stop in front of a FOR SALE sign.

Behind the sign was a three-story neo-Gothic structure of dark red brick, with a clock tower in the middle, gable windows on the top story, and high pavilions on the east and west corners.

It had to be at least twenty thousand square feet.

"We can't afford it," said Reggie.

"I don't want to buy it," said Laura. "I only want to visit. This was my school."

Laura was already getting out of the car before Reggie had even set the brake. She walked across unkempt grass to the main entrance—a heavy oaken double door beneath the clock tower.

The door was more than locked. It was shielded now with an iron grate and an estate agent's lockbox.

Laura sighed and stepped back.

"I went to school, too," said Reggie, "but I've never been tempted to relive it."

"We'll have better luck if we try the back," said Laura.

She didn't wait for Reggie to object. He had to run to catch up as she walked quickly around the side of the east pavilion.

At the back, the two pavilions had been extended to form a courtyard, which was closed off from the adjacent meadow—what once had been the school's playing field—by a simple iron gate. It was secured by the cheapest sort of padlock from the local hardware store.

"What do you think?" said Laura. "Just break it? Or shall we try to climb over?"

"I can pick it, if you really want," said Reggie. "Barristers do learn skills from their clients. But why? What's in here?"

"The Winter Holiday Dance. My very first dance," said Laura, with a look on her face that Reggie could not fathom at all. He wanted to decipher it.

So he picked the lock. It clicked loose.

They stepped inside the gymnasium. It was almost pitch-dark, too dark to proceed without a light.

"I expect the power is on," said Reggie, "since they have to show the place to prospective buyers."

Laura reached for a switch on the side wall, as though she remembered exactly where it should be—and it was. Overhead lights flickered and then came on, several at a time, with a hum in the otherwise-silent room.

The bleachers on either side were contracted, up tight against the walls. There was dust on the gym floor, but even so, the shine of the heavy varnish glinted back at the lights.

"This is where we had all the dances. I was very awkward at the first one. I was quite awkward at the last one as well, but then, I was only at school here long enough for three."

"Too bad we don't have music," said Reggie. "But I could put my mobile on speaker mode."

"No. Somehow I don't think that will quite do."

"Should I whistle?"

"No. I've heard you whistle."

"Well, if there's no music for dancing, and you won't let me whistle, what is there to do?"

"Oh, I could think of something. But what if the estate agent is showing the place today?"

"That would be a bonus for them, I suppose."

"We'll just dance quietly. If you are more ambitious than that, you'll just have to wait and hope for the best."

"Fair enough."

They began to slow-dance. Reggie was careful not to whistle and spoil the mood. After a moment, Laura said, "You know, the first time I danced with a boy who reacted to me this way—"

"What way?"

"The way you're reacting; don't try to be coy about it. I got so embarrassed that I ran from the room crying."

"You're not going to do that now, are you?"

"Perhaps. Why don't you kiss me first, and then we'll just see—"

Laura stopped suddenly.

"What?" asked Reggie.

"Did you hear that? That banging noise. Like someone slamming a—"

Now there was a sound that even Reggie heard.

"Must be the wind rattled a pipe somehow," he said. "Or maybe a heating system, or—"

"I think it's time we go," said Laura. "It could be an estate agent. Or worse, paparazzi."

"But—"

Laura disengaged.

"Now don't make me call the chaperone," she said. "C'mon, I'll race you back to the car."

With no further discussion, they exited the gym. Reggie closed the door behind them and listened for a moment, but he heard nothing more like the sound from earlier.

They ran around the pavilion and back to the front of the school.

They made it to the MGB and jumped in without encountering paparazzi or anyone else.

Probably an estate agent had just brought someone by for a quick outside look, suggested Laura.

That seemed unlikely to Reggie, but it didn't matter. He started the car and drove quickly on the way home, wanting as much time alone with Laura as possible before she had to go back to rehearsal.

Late that afternoon, after slow dancing led to other things back at the house, Laura sighed and got up from the bed.

She knew from the snoring that Reggie was asleep. She could nudge him and tell him to stop, and thereby get a nap herself.

Or she could take advantage of the snoring, knowing that as long as it continued, her absence would be undetected.

She put on her robe and went out on the balcony.

She heard water running in a stream somewhere. No wind whatsoever; the pine trees were misty and absolutely still.

Laura had not made many mistakes in her life. At least none worth dwelling on, which was how she measured such things. But anyone watching now as she stood at the balcony railing, just staring out at the still trees, would have thought she was dwelling on one now.

And perhaps someone was watching. Because the snoring had stopped.

Laura quickly turned and looked toward Reggie in the bed. False alarm. He was still asleep. He had just turned slightly onto his side, and so the snoring had paused. His eyes were closed and he was breathing evenly. That was nice.

Still in her robe, Laura quietly picked up her purse, put on slippers, pushed the door open, and went downstairs.

She sat at the kitchen table and took a folded sheet of paper out of her purse. She unfolded it in front of her, read it, and stared at it for a long moment. Then she picked it up and looked at the other side. She turned it again and looked closely at each of the corners. She held it up to the light.

But all of that revealed nothing. She put the letter flat on the table in front of her, read it once more, and sighed.

Now she heard a noise. She looked up.

At the top of the stairs, Reggie stood looking back down at Laura as she sat at the kitchen table. Light through the kitchen window had a translucent effect on her silk gown, and that was the first thing he had noticed. But what he was noticing now was what she had laid out before her on the table, and the tension in her face as she stared at it.

"What's that?" asked Reggie.

Laura immediately put her hand on the unfolded sheet of paper she had been staring at. But she could hardly cover it completely, and she resisted the impulse to try to stuff it back in her purse.

"Script changes?" asked Reggie as he pulled up a chair.

"Ah . . . no," said Laura. "I mean . . . I tried not to wake you."

Reggie looked at the words that were visible between Laura's fingers.

"'Dear Mr. Sherlock Holmes—'" he began to read. Then: "What the—"

"Now, I can explain," said Laura quickly. "I know you aren't fond of these . . . kinds of letters. The only reason I put a copy in my bag is because—"

"We have staff for these things," said Reggie. "And for good reason. What's one doing popping up on our honeymoon?"

"I . . . It was nothing, really. I was at Baker Street Chambers, you know, that last day in London before the wedding, and I'd just gotten off the phone with you, and I had to get rid of Mr. Rafferty; then I went into your office and changed clothes, and when I came out, I saw that I had accidentally knocked one of the letters onto the floor, and so I picked it up, and—well, this is it!"

Reggie stared at Laura, not just perplexed but also astonished. He had never seen her get a hand caught in any sort of cookie jar, much less make excuses about it.

"I wanted to tell you, Reggie," she continued, "and I was going to. I just . . . I just kept putting it off because I know how much you want nothing to do with the letters anymore. You remember what you said before we left London?"

"Yes. I remember my rant. I said I wanted nothing more to do with the bloody letters. I also said I never wanted to see another bloody paparazzo as long as I lived. I even said I didn't want to see another bloody solicitor and client walk in at Baker Street Chambers ever again.

But of course what I meant in all that was just that I wanted the whole bloody world to get lost so that I could be with you."

Laura looked at him.

"I wish you wouldn't say things to me like that when I have to get dressed for rehearsal," she said.

Reggie ignored that for the moment, and he slid the letter from under Laura's fingertips. It read as follows:

Dear Mr. Sherlock Holmes:

I swore a solemn vow not to tell a single living soul. But it is said that you are a character of fiction. And therefore not a living soul. I can tell you, then, without breaking my vow:

Something is terribly wrong in Bodfyn. Please send Scarecrow.

"'Something is terribly wrong in Bodfyn,'" repeated Reggie, musing over it.

"Yes," said Laura.

"Aside from the name of the place," said Reggie.

"Of course," said Laura.

Reggie frowned and sat down at the table.

"I can understand why you picked this letter up. I understand why you put it in your purse. And I understand now why you brought us here, I do—you care about this weird little place. And about your friend and mentor,

Mrs. Hatfield. What I don't understand is how on earth this letter managed to come to you."

"As I said, I was waiting for you at Baker Street, and—"

"Yes, but what I mean is, what sort of coincidence can it be that a letter about Bodfyn—a town of fewer than two hundred people—could arrive at Baker Street Chambers, addressed to Sherlock Holmes, just at the right moment for you to happen to see it?"

"A nearly impossible coincidence?"

"Yes," said Reggie. "That's what worries me. I don't believe the letter, I don't believe most of them, and I wouldn't have done anything to check this one out because I don't give a rat's ass about the town in any case. But you do. And it arrived in perfect timing for you to be there to receive it."

"I can't explain it, either," said Laura. "But there it was. What was I to do?"

Reggie had no answer; he just shook his head.

Laura started back up the stairs.

"Where are you going? I think we need to figure this out."

"I do, too," said Laura. "But I need to get dressed. I have to go back now for one more run-through."

"Bloody hell. Can't you just tell them no?"

"Really, Reggie. I can't let them all down. I'll have to go. But I'll be just a couple of hours. We've had such a wonderful day. Don't make me feel bad about it now. Why don't you just go back to the pub? Have a pint or two. Play some darts. Like you used to do."

"You mean like when I was single and had nothing better to do?"

She kissed him quickly on the lips.

"I'll be back before midnight. I promise. Just don't turn them into a pumpkin while I'm gone."

10

At the pub, Charlie, the same bartender from the night before, came over to pour Reggie's beer.

Reggie just stared at the counter, too worried to look up.

"Foster's," said Reggie.

"Just the one?" asked Charlie.

"For a start," said Reggie.

The bartender poured the Foster's, gave a conspicuous glance at the empty bar stool next to Reggie, and got a look on his face that could only be described as gloating.

Reggie focused on his beer, took a long draft, and when he finally glanced up, he was annoyed to see the man still standing there.

"What?" asked Reggie.

"You and the lady were here."

Reggie nodded.

"I'm trying to remember," the bartender continued.

"It was last night," said Reggie.

"No," said the bartender. "I mean, why she looks familiar. Like someone from the cinema, I think."

Reggie rubbed his forehead. He didn't need this. If the bartender recognized Laura, and phoned in a tip, the paparazzi would descend on them in worse fashion than if they had not attempted to travel incognito at all.

No answer was safe.

"Seems unlikely," said Reggie lightly, as if the man had been joking.

"Don't see how you would know who I went to the cinema with back in the day," said the man. He gave Reggie a defiant look, and then he turned away and went through the doors to the back kitchen.

Reggie was too preoccupied to wonder about that reaction. In fact, he was glad the bartender was gone. He had Laura's letter in his pocket, and he took it out now for another look. He was worried.

The lack of a signature bothered him. The urgency of the summons bothered him.

Most of all, it bothered him that whoever had sent it knew that Laura Rankin was Scarecrow from Bodfyn.

How else could they have imagined the letter would get to her? And how did they know she would be there to receive it? They would almost have had to hand-deliver it while she was there.

That letters written to Sherlock Holmes would get delivered and read at Baker Street Chambers was common knowledge. *The Daily Sun* had made sure of that over the past few years—always in a way designed to embarrass Reggie Heath.

That Laura Rankin was marrying Reggie Heath of Baker Street Chambers was also common knowledge.

But it was not common knowledge that Laura was Scarecrow. He himself had not known that until today.

And other than Mrs. Hatfield, Reggie did not know of anyone who knew all those things and also had a reason to summon Laura that was both urgent and benign. In his experience, urgency by definition usually suggested at least the possibility of a consequence that was not benign.

He didn't like it. He didn't know quite what was going on, but whatever it was, he didn't like doing nothing about it.

He took out his mobile phone, intending to call Baker Street Chambers. But Mrs. Hatfield was right: He got no bars at all. It was a dead zone. He also couldn't ring Laura to check on her. He would get no reception unless an unknown satellite, the clouds, and the stars should all align.

Reggie grabbed his mac, went outside, and began walking toward the theater at the opposite end of town. True, his previous visit there had been a disaster, and probably everyone was onstage and would regard his presence as an intrusion.

Still, he would check. He walked quickly up the street. And, as sometimes happened, the more Reggie walked, the more clearly he was able to think (or so he felt). It was still light out, and there were locals about, visiting the grocer, the tea shop, the estate agent—quite a normal little town, really. What sort of jeopardy Laura could possibly be in was not apparent. He was probably worried about nothing.

By the time he reached the theater, he was almost in good spirits. He walked up the pavers to the entrance. He could hear voices from inside. The door was locked, but he put his ear to it.

"Out, damned spot!"

Yes, that was Laura's voice, clear as a bell. If nothing else, he knew she was fine. He could relax.

He turned and began walking back toward the pub.

He passed the estate agent's office along the way, with its listings of properties for sale posted in the window. He paused. He recognized one; it was a glossy picture and detailed listing for Laura's former boarding school.

Just as Reggie stopped to look, the door opened and a crying woman stepped out.

It was Mrs. Hatfield.

She saw Reggie, started to turn away, then gave up on that and settled on just putting a silk handkerchief to her face.

"Oh. This is so embarrassing," she said.

"Are you all right?"

"Yes, yes, I . . . I'm fine. I just . . . have been such a fool."

She looked very much as though she would tear up again.

"Let me buy you a cup of tea," said Reggie.

She nodded. The tearoom was only two doors away and still open. They went right in, sat down, and got a pot of Earl Grey and a plate of vanilla biscuits.

"Is there . . . something wrong at the theater?" asked Reggie. "I was just there, but of course I was careful not to intrude."

"Oh, no, not at all," said Mrs. Hatfield. She managed a smile. "The play is coming along splendidly. Thanks to your wife, young man. We're doing the final dress right now. We will be ready to open tomorrow night, no question."

"Then why, if I may ask, are you . . ."

"Because it is going so splendidly," said Mrs. Hatfield, "and everyone in town has bought tickets and is coming tomorrow, absolutely everyone, and so I know it is going to be such a success . . ."

"Yes?"

"That I came to talk to the estate agent today about the school. About how much it will take. So I will know how close we are getting in the fund-raising, and . . . and . . ."

"And?"

She got her sniffles under control and looked directly at Reggie.

"We might as well be having a bake sale to send a man to the moon!"

"Oh."

Reggie could offer nothing else. Of course a community theater's weekend play could not raise enough money for a down payment on such a property. That should have been obvious from the start.

"Was there . . . some sort of commitment made? Did you have a previous discussion with the estate agent?"

"Oh, no, not me; I left that to Mr. Turner. I only came in today because I was just so excited about how well it was going, and I thought . . . Oh, I don't know what I was thinking. Poor Mr. Turner, he will be so disappointed."

"I take it that he believed you could raise enough money?"

"Oh yes. He was certain of it. He said that our little play this weekend would . . . would make it possible to buy the school, open it again, and save the town itself!"

Reggie was silent for a moment. He hadn't given it much thought at all—it was Bodfyn's business, after all—but the entire plan was highly unlikely. Even if the money were raised, the property would never be a school again. It was simply too far now from the population centers.

"You've still staged a wonderful play, Mrs. Hatfield, I'm sure. That's something to be proud of. It's a shame if someone gave you unrealistic advice."

"Oh, no, it's our own fault. Mr. Turner's and mine. He was so sure; he did so much research on it, he told me. But what do we know? We're just a couple of sad and foolish old academics!"

"No, Mrs. Hatfield, you are not. I don't know anything else about you, but I know that you are Laura's mentor. And in my opinion, there is nothing sad or foolish about that."

She began to recover a little now.

"Thank you," she said. "I suppose I'd better be going back to the theater now."

She got up from the table; Reggie paid the bill and walked outside with her.

"Would you like to join me, and see the final rehearsal of the last act?" she asked.

"No, thank you very much," said Reggie. "I thought I would just go down to the pub and . . . get to know it a little better."

"That's fine, dear. You just go and have a good time. And take a look through that telescope, too!"

She turned away toward the theater, and Reggie went on toward the pub, feeling a little conflicted. On first meeting Mrs. Hatfield, he admitted to himself, he had found her just a bit annoying; that was because she seemed to be the cause of an infringement on his time with Laura.

But seeing her cry in front of the estate agent's—which, he noticed, was closed now as he walked by—made him feel quite differently. Someone, somehow, had misled the woman. Estate agents had been known to do that, sometimes with their clients never realizing it. If Reggie's mobile had any reception at all—he took it out of his pocket now and checked again; still nothing—he would have called his brother, Nigel, who was quite good at ferreting out that sort of thing, and put him onto it.

But he could reach no one. And before he could rest easy about Laura, there was still something he needed to know.

Reggie put his phone away and continued on to the pub.

11

There were some new early evening patrons at the Wayward Pony.

A man in poorly chosen casual business clothes was in a back booth, looking at advertising flyers. Probably the estate agent, fresh from the office. In another booth was an older couple, too carefully attired to be local, who were just now being joined by a younger woman, who was too casual not to be.

Reggie went to the bar, hoping to get the bartender talking on the right subject this time. But he saw only the barmaid. She came over and drew his beer.

"Where did the bartender go?" said Reggie.

"Fixing something in the kitchen," she said, as she poured Reggie's beer. "You were here last night, weren't you? You and the lady. The stand-in for Melanie."

"Yes. Say, perhaps you can tell me—just what sort of accident was it that happened to Melanie?"

"Fell into one of the quarries."

"Quarries?"

"On the moor. They used to cut granite here. She wasn't found until the next morning. The coroner drove out from Amesbury to rule on it."

"Did he say how one falls into a quarry?"

"Don't know. Gravity? Maybe she tripped taking a selfie? I was going to replace her, you know. I mean, not that I would push anyone into a quarry for a role."

"No, of course not."

"Anyway, it's your lady that takes the role now."

"Yes. Well. I am sorry about that."

"Maybe she pushed Melanie?"

"What? No! I wasn't suggesting anyone pushed anyone! I was just curious."

"Hmm. It was all in our local paper, you know."

"I don't suppose you'd still have a copy?"

"We have a recycle bin, just like anyone else."

"Can you check? I'd very much appreciate it?"

She frowned, but nodded.

"I'll ask Charlie," she said, and she went away to the back kitchen.

Now, the three people who had been sitting at the nearby booth came up to join Reggie—a portly white-haired man of about seventy, in an expensive London-casual sport coat and a narrow woolen tie; a woman of the right age and attire to be his wife; and a twentyish woman in jeans and a faded logo pullover.

"We know you!" said the man, clapping a hand on Reggie's shoulder.

The two women sat on the bar chairs on either side, flanking Reggie.

"You do?" said Reggie. "I'm sorry, I can't quite place you."

"We met in London, certainly," said the gentleman.

This was worrisome. Had they met in some capacity at the Old Bailey? If so, Reggie's being recognized now would not be an issue by itself, but once that was established, the connection to Laura would not be far behind.

He resorted to his barrister's training and tried to confuse the issue.

"Have you been to Piccadilly Circus?" asked Reggie. "Perhaps we bumped into each other there?"

"Well, of course I've been to Piccadilly Circus," said the gentleman. "So has much of the civilized world. But there are always a million people there, so I could hardly remember you out of all of them."

"Ah," said Reggie. "You are mistaken, then. We don't know each other after all. No harm done. I hope you enjoy your stay here."

Reggie tried to turn away on his bar stool, but the man's tipsy wife blocked him.

"My husband is a highly renowned archaeologist, I'll have you know!" she announced.

"Now, dear, don't make a fuss—"

"He was with the British Museum!"

"Ahh, Perhaps that's where you saw me, then; I was there once," said Reggie. "At the museum, I mean."

"Excellent! What was your particular interest?"

"T. rex, at the time. It was a school field trip. I was eight."

"Oh. Well, that's not why you look familiar, then, is it? But I'm sure in time it will come to me."

Reggie tried to change the subject.

"So, you are an archaeologist? Are you on a dig here?"

The man laughed.

"Not at all. We're on holiday. Just plain old tourists!"

"And I'm their tour guide!" said the younger woman, much further along in her cups than the other two.

"I thought perhaps you were collecting antiquities or something for the museum," said Reggie to the archaeologist.

The man laughed again at the apparent absurdity of it.

"Not a bit of it; this area was fully explored a couple of decades ago, nothing to be found. Not even King Arthur's funeral pyre!" Now he grinned and slapped a hand on Reggie's back. "Truth is, for my wife and me, at our age, I feel that every time we return to the museum, we're bringing them antiquities!"

"Speak for yourself, you old coot!" said the wife.

"And I'm their tour guide!"

The young woman announced this with even greater drunken enthusiasm than before. She waved an arm around to indicate the whole expanse of everything for which she was to be their guide, and then she would have fallen dizzily to the floor if Reggie had not propped her up against the bar.

The archaeologist tried once more.

"You really do look familiar to me. Something missing, though. Do you wear a hairpiece, usually?"

Reggie took a moment to be depressed that his hairline—just recently having begun to recede, and really hardly at all—had become that noticeable.

"Maybe what's missing is the lady from the other night," said the young woman, having recovered her balance, and a bit of belligerence. "That so-called actress."

"Oh?" said the archaeologist. "Anyone we've heard of?"

"Probably not," said Reggie. "Well. Don't let me keep you!"

Reggie stood, clapped the man on the shoulder, and then quickly turned back to the bar.

Reluctantly, the couple finally exited, along with their cheerful tour guide.

Reggie got up from the bar and walked to the back booth, where the estate agent was seated, with several glossy land-sales brochures spread out on the table.

"May I join you for a moment?" asked Reggie.

The man looked up and saw that Reggie looked like he had the money to be a buyer.

"Certainly," he said.

Reggie sat down and pointed at the brochures.

"Do you know the area well?" he asked.

"Better than most," said the agent.

"What can you tell me about the old boarding school out on A30?"

"I can tell you that two hundred years ago it was not a boarding school at all, but a lavishly custom-built estate—and that is what it will soon be once more. Are you interested?"

"Not exactly in that way," said Reggie. "I'm wondering what you would say about the chances of someone buying it and returning it to its educational purpose?"

The agent looked surprised.

"You are the second person to ask me about that today," he said.

"Is it an unusual question?"

"Well, I . . . I would say that yes, it is. You and a woman earlier today are the only ones who have inquired regarding such a use for the property."

"Really?" said Reggie. "No one else has inquired along those lines at all?"

"No. And I doubt that anyone will. The property is simply worth more as an estate. I don't think anyone could afford it as a school. Fifty years or a hundred years ago, this was a viable location for a boarding school, but not two years ago when it closed, and not now."

"I see," said Reggie. "And yet there is a fund-raiser in this town for that purpose."

The agent sighed.

"Yes, I know," he said. "But it only started up just recently, after she began work on fixing up the local theater. I took it to be just a sort of promotional tactic—you know, to get everyone enthused to attend the opening night. In that respect, of course, it worked. My understanding is that literally everyone in this town is going."

"Even you?"

"Of course. I don't want to lose potential clients. At this point, not to go would be an affront."

Reggie nodded. He looked at the brochures spread out on the table and politely remarked that some of the properties were situated in quite striking landscapes.

"Yes," said the estate agent. "Location, location, location. That's what everything is about."

"So they say," said Reggie.

"And it applies to everything. This pub, for example. It's the only place in town where you can just look out from your deck and see the moor. Best location there is."

"You mean in terms of property values, correct?"

The estate agent shrugged.

"Depends on how you feel about the moor, I guess,"

he said. "Some people like to say that timing is everything. Personally, I put my money on location."

"Well, I suppose it's all relative," said Reggie, and he stood up now, because he saw that the barmaid had returned and was looking for him. She came over to the booth.

"Charlie said to tell you that the recycle bin was full this week, so he just tossed the papers in the Dumpster, and that you are welcome to knock yourself out. Which he said he hopes you do. Not sure why he said that."

"I see," said Reggie. "And where is—"

"The Dumpster is out back, below the deck. I'll pour you a fresh beer when you come back, but you'll probably want to wash your hands first. And maybe change your shirt."

12

Reggie found the Dumpster by the smell of it.

He also saw that there was still room in the nearby recycling box for much more newspaper. Judging from the cut twine, Reggie's guess was that the bartender had actually transferred the more recent papers to the Dumpster just for Reggie's benefit.

That didn't matter. Reggie opened the Dumpster lid, to the visceral stench of rotting vegetables and burnt cooking oil.

There were no newspapers on top of the pile. Of course not, that would have been too easy. He would have to dig, probably wherever it was most unpleasant. That would be the side with discarded fish parts.

Reggie rolled up his sleeves and plunged in above the elbows. Yes, there it was—the bartender had literally used it as fish wrap. Reggie pulled the dripping parcel from the bin and shook out the entrails.

On an inside page, under the heading "Quarry Victim Drowned," he found a summary of the coroner's findings.

A hiking accident at dusk. A woman who had walked out too far to get back before dark, was too absorbed in her music to pay attention, and had fallen into an abandoned quarry and drowned.

The newspaper dutifully included a map, showing the location of the particular quarry on the moor. It was beyond the hill behind the theater.

Reggie tore that one soggy page from the paper and returned to the deck behind the pub. He looked out toward the moor.

The sun was setting. There wasn't time to walk back to the theater and start from there. If he wanted to see where the accident had happened while there was still any light at all, he would have to take the shortest route, and cut diagonally across the moor, and do so immediately. No time for another beer.

Reggie came down from the deck, walked around the side of the pub, then down the slope where the viewing deck jutted out, and then up the opposite slope. He zipped up his mac, edged his way through a hedgerow of thorny gorse bushes, and then set out rapidly across the moor.

He was not nearly so much a fan of nature walks as

Laura was. He knew, as the wind picked up and stirred the grasses, and the setting sun glinted on the pinkish heather and on the yellow gorse flowers and on the white stones that were embedded pretty much everywhere in the mud, that this should be a pleasant walk. No mystery as to why the unfortunate hiker had gone out.

On the other hand, the stirring grasses bristled with edges like razors; the yellow gorse bushes had stabbing thorns that were longer and harder than those on any rose or bougainvillea; the rocks impeded his stride and stubbed his toes from their hiding places in the mud; and the breeze was getting damn cold.

He wanted to get this over with, satisfy his nagging doubt, loop back to civilization at the theater, where Laura was rehearsing, and then just take her home.

He kept his eye on the tor—the white granite outcropping—at the top of the hill that rose up behind the theater. According to the newspaper, the woman had stumbled on the slope just below that.

The tor was a natural structure, not man-made, he knew. But if the forces of nature had not created it there, humans would have—it was that good a landmark. Exactly where anyone out for a hike—or walking on the moor for any reason—would want to head.

He was almost there, but he was finding his way in twilight. He quickened his pace.

Now he was at the summit, right next to the tor. To his left, the ground sloped down to the field behind the theater. To his right, some fifty yards farther onto the moor, was where the woman was said to have fallen.

He descended the slope cautiously, trying not to disturb rocks and mud that could ruin whatever evidence might still be there—and trying not to slide down the slope and into the quarry himself.

With just a few yards to go, Reggie stopped.

He was already too late, he knew, to learn much of anything. The light was fading very quickly now, and Reggie knew he would not be able to find anything at dusk that the coroner had not found in full daylight.

But any coroner, no matter how good, investigates far more natural and accidental deaths than intentional ones. It would be difficult not to assume that this was just another accident.

Reggie could make the opposite assumption. And he had to, because he had to understand the letter that had brought Laura here. If something was terribly wrong in Bodfyn, surely it had to do with the death of this young woman. Why it should involve Laura, he didn't know—but it did involve her. Or at least the letter writer thought it did.

So if it had not been an accident—if the woman had not fallen into the quarry, but had been pushed—where would that person have stood?

Reggie walked several yards back up the slope. One possibility—given that the woman had been wearing headphones—was that someone had simply followed her on the path and come up behind her, unheard and un-seen. If that had been the case, then Reggie knew he would find nothing—any obvious footprints would have been no-ticed by the coroner, any remaining ones were likely obliterated by now, and Reggie would not be able to find them in the dark in any case.

But what if, instead of pursuing from behind, someone had lain in wait?

There were yellow gorse bushes on both sides of the path, just two or three yards from the edge of the quarry, still just picking up enough light to be visible. Reggie went to the nearest one and inspected it as closely as he could. The thorns grabbed at his mac and pricked his hands. He found nothing.

He went to the next. The breeze picked up, and he thought he saw something move. He bent down, scratch-ing his neck on a thorn—but he found it. A piece of tweed cloth, dark brown. A man's coat, probably.

Someone had gone to the trouble of hiding in a damn gorse bush and waiting until the young woman had gotten close enough to the edge.

And then she had been pushed.

13

It was night as Reggie came down the slope, past the windbreak of pine trees, and into the parking area at the back of the former church.

He heard nothing as he arrived, but probably that was just because they were on break.

He didn't want to breach etiquette yet again by going in through the back; he walked around to the front entrance.

The exterior light was on. He knocked at the front door. No answer. No answer the second time, either.

He tried the door. Locked.

He checked his watch. Nearly nine.

Fair enough. Dress rehearsal must have been completed, and everyone had adjourned to the pub.

Reggie started up the main road in that direction.

It was a bloody inconvenience not to have cell phone

reception. He wanted to call Laura; probably she had gone to the pub with everyone else, but she might just have walked back to the house.

At least it was on the way. When he reached the house, he ran up to the entrance, unlocked the door, looked in, and called out.

No answer.

So she must have gone on to the pub.

Reggie walked quickly down the main street.

As he neared the pub, it became obvious that was where everyone had gone. The interior lights blazed out through the windows and lit up the street; he could hear rowdy singing fifty yards away.

Surely all was fine and wonderful.

He made up his mind not to tell anyone but Laura where he had gone and what he had found. He was beginning to have his own doubts about it now anyway as he approached the cheery sight and sound of the pub. In any case, all he needed right now was to see Laura.

He opened the door—carefully, in case any drunk people should spill out. But none did, and he went inside.

He had hoped to see Laura at the bar, having a pint and waiting to greet him, but she wasn't. A couple of locals who were at the bar glanced briefly in his direction, then went back to a loud discussion of a football match on the telly.

The bartender wasn't there; two barmaids were handling everything.

The singing was coming from the area of the back booth, where most of the people in costume had gathered, taking over several tables and chairs, as well. They seemed to have reached the end of a refrain, and now most of them burst out laughing.

Reggie walked directly over, expecting to see Laura seated in the booth.

But, again, she wasn't.

The director was there, chatting drunkenly with the prop mistress and three witches. Macbeth and a couple of other Scottish warlords, minus swords and armor, were there as well, doing their best to impress some local women who had been lured in by the festivities.

The director finally looked up at Reggie.

"Where is she?" asked Reggie.

"Who?" said the director, in mock confusion. "Or which? A witch?"

The director's companions broke up in laughter.

Reggie put his hands on the table and leaned in.

"My wife."

The director managed to focus semisoberly for a moment, and then he shook his head and shrugged.

"Is Mrs. Hatfield here?"

The director considered that, rolled his eyes, and shrugged again.

Reggie pushed the man's beer away.

"Give me an actual answer. Now. Did Laura leave the theater with you?"

The director improved his focus enough now to actually speak.

"No. They were both still at the theater when the rest of us left."

Reggie stepped back from the table, looked about him once more for anyone who might possibly have any information, and then exited the pub.

He ran down the street to the theater. Now there were no lights on at all, no cars parked, no people. The banner was there, flapping in the breeze at one corner where it had come loose. He heard the sound of that, and of his own footsteps on the pavement, and nothing else.

He went to the entrance. The heavy wooden door was still closed, but when he tried the latch, it turned.

He pushed the door open.

It was completely dark inside. He groped on the wall until he found the switch.

The lamps from the side walls came on, but nothing overhead. It would have been enough for parishioners or theatergoers to find their way through the pews, but it was not enough to tell at a glance whether anyone else was there.

The converted stage at the far end was still in shadows. Reggie walked quickly toward it, down the center aisle.

"Laura?" he called out as he walked, but he was nearly certain already that no one was there. He glanced at the pew rows a couple of times as he walked past them. It occurred to him that perhaps this was all just some sort of joke that the theater group was playing on the non-theaterish outsider. They were, after all, in his experience (with the exception of Laura, of course), rather strange people.

But no. He reached the stage, and no one had jumped out from the pews to yell "Surprise."

He was growing just a little annoyed. He didn't bother to go around to the steps on either side; he just jumped up directly onto the middle of the stage.

The sound of that echoed, but nothing else made a peep. He looked behind one of the side curtains, fumbled around again, and finally flipped the stage switch.

Bright lights came on, blinding at first, and when he stopped blinking, he saw that the stage set was more or less complete. If he had taken another step in before getting the lights on, he would have tripped over a plastic prop that was undoubtedly meant to represent a chamber pot.

He hoped none of the cast members had gotten over-enthusiastic about the Method acting approach.

In the center of the stage was a king-size—well, yes, of course it was—bed. The set was obviously the royal bedchamber.

No, Lady Macbeth was not in the bed.

Pity. If that had been the joke, and Laura the one playing it on him, he would have forgiven the sense of anxiety he was beginning to feel. No harm in getting the adrenaline up, after all, if for a good purpose.

But no. Laura was not here. Reggie took out his mobile, saw that he had some minimal reception, and tried again to ring her, but he received no answer.

Reggie searched urgently through his phone list to see if Laura had given him Mrs. Hatfield's number. She had; there it was. His phone still showed one bar. He rang her, waited—and waited—and then, mercifully, the call went through and she picked up.

"This is Reggie Heath, Mrs. Hatfield. I'm looking for Laura."

A surprised silence, then: "And so . . . why are you calling me, dear?"

"You and she were the last ones at rehearsal."

"Yes, I think that's true, but she left before I did. Have you tried the pub?"

"Of course. Everyone else is there, but Laura is not."

"Oh," said Mrs. Hatfield. "Well, if she isn't with you, and not with the cast, and not at the house, I suppose that is a little odd."

"Yes," said Reggie.

"But I'm sure it must just be some sort of misunderstanding, is all. Now, I don't want to pry, but—I don't suppose the two of you . . . you didn't have a little quarrel of some kind, did you?"

"Of course not," said Reggie. "Well, I mean, nothing that would—look, I just know that is not it."

"Of course, if you say so."

"I do. And . . . Mrs. Hatfield, is there a reason why you yourself are not at the pub with the cast?"

"Well, yes, dear, as a matter of fact. After talking with you earlier today, I began to . . . wonder about some things. I rang my old colleague from the school, Mr. Turner, who's been so encouraging about the play and raising the funds and so on. I was going to meet up with him in a few minutes, but—honestly, dear, if you are worried about Laura, then I am, too, and that takes priority. Where are you now?"

"At the theater. On the stage, to be precise."

"Really? How did you get in?"

"I walked in. The door was unlocked."

"Oh goodness. Not hanging wide open, I hope, was it?"

"No. But unlocked."

"Well. That was silly of me. I was the last to leave. I should have been more careful. Well. Did I remember to turn the lights out at least?"

"I presume so. Nothing was on when I came in."

"And no one else there at all?"

"No."

"Did you check backstage? The dressing area?"

"Why would anyone be backstage with all the lights off?"

"Yes, yes, good point. Well then. I'll meet you straightaway at your house. Not at the theater—it's such an uncomfortable place. The house would be better, don't you think?"

"All right," said Reggie. "How long will you be?"

"I have my car; I can be there in ten minutes. That will give you time to walk back, I suppose?"

"Yes."

"Very well. I'm sure everything is fine. In fact, I'll bet Laura will be there by the time you get back. Not to worry. Now, do me a favor, dear, and lock up as you leave, won't you?"

Reggie agreed to do that.

But first he stepped behind the curtains and went backstage. He found the light switch for the one room that served for props, makeup, and everything else. He turned the lights on, and found nothing. So far as he could tell, it was all normal.

He went to Laura's makeup station and saw his own worried expression in the mirror. He knew next to nothing about theater makeup, but he could see that she had used the makeup remover—and then had not put it back or even closed the makeup case.

He left the room and went back into the main part of the theater, accidentally kicking a sword as he walked across the stage. He locked up, left the theater, and walked back into the street, now headed home, his hard shoes echoing on the wet cobblestones. He mulled over what Mrs. Hatfield had said. There were any number of explanations for Laura's absence. True, he was not fond of any that he'd been able to imagine, but that didn't mean that there was not a perfectly benign explanation. He, in his bullheaded emotional state, had just not been able to think of one.

And of course he couldn't call in the district constabulary for a grown woman who had been missing for all of two hours. After all, it wasn't as though she was out in the wilderness and in danger of dying of exposure.

Was it? There was that wide field beyond the garden behind the house. . . .

Reggie was in front of the house now. The kitchen light was still off, which he regarded as a pretty certain indicator that Laura had not returned. The front porch lamp was on, but he had left it that way.

There was just enough light from it that now it occurred to him that he had not done the most obvious thing. Quite naturally, of course, because when he had left the house, he wasn't thinking of Laura as being missing.

But now he was. And he saw that the ground both in front and all around the house was soft, except for that one portion of incomplete walkway—and there was just enough light to look.

He stopped in his tracks, and began to look for Laura's.

He was standing just at the edge of the muddy patch that a person had to walk through to get from the end of the cobblestone walkway to the paved street.

He could still see his own tracks in that mud from ear-lier, and traces of the mud where he had tracked it into the street and it had not yet been drizzled away.

He did not see Laura's. And although she was much better at not stepping in things unintentionally than he was, he could see no way in which she could have gotten onto the street without walking in the mud. Even Laura could not have done that.

So Reggie began to check for tracks around the entire house. He started where the cobblestone walkway crossed the garden border and proceeded to his right.

He reached the side yard, having seen no signs of any-one's being there before him. He looked back at where he had just stepped and saw that indeed he was leaving clear prints—surely Laura would have, too.

He fished into his coat pocket for his key chain, onto which he had attached a tiny LED torch, something he did whenever he traveled. There had been times when he wanted one on his journeys with Laura.

He continued down along the side yard toward the back of the house.

There was a momentary break in the clouds as he neared the end of the side yard. Some sixty or seventy yards distant he could just make out the dark profile of the hedgerow that separated the backyard of the house from the meadow and farming fields beyond.

Still no footprints or anything else. He turned the

corner to continue around the back just as the clouds closed ranks again, and even the slightest moonlight was gone.

Reggie pushed the button on the LED torch and pointed it directly at the muddy path in front of him, bending slightly for a better look. He could see little else, and he paid attention to nothing around him but the damp cold that had begun to creep in underneath his collar and through his shoes.

There were no footprints. He still saw nothing.

Just then, for a moment, he thought heard something. It sounded mechanical, and so far distant that he couldn't really be sure. It seemed to be coming from somewhere out beyond the fields and stand of trees.

The coughing of fuel igniting, a backfire, sputtering—slowly and then more rapidly and surely—and then the sound of an engine fully alive.

Not a car, thought Reggie. Not a motorcycle.

A plane. A small plane.

He looked in that direction—he was almost sure the sound was coming from where he and Laura had flown in—but of course he could see nothing from where he was.

He wanted to run in the direction of that sound, to make sure it was not what first came into his mind, but it would be much too far on foot.

Then some instinct made him look down again, and a few meters in front of him, he saw something.

Not a footprint, but something of a bright color, a

glimpse of cloth—of familiar clothing, dear God—and Reggie redirected the circumference of the torch light a bit to one side—and then he froze.

In an instant, he was on his hands and knees over the prostrate female form. He didn't remember to breathe as he reached for her.

Then a shiver of intense pain went up the back of his head, and everything went black.

14

TWO HOURS EARLIER

Final dress rehearsal was done, and Laura was at the backstage mirror, finally able to take her makeup off.

The rehearsal had gone well enough. There were dropped lines and mishandled cues and stumbles and early exits by a few of the players, but it was community theater, after all, and it was for a good cause. Laura had no complaints.

Mrs. Hatfield, who had watched from the front row, had seemed a bit distracted while giving her stage notes after—but perhaps that was just Laura's imagination. After all, she felt a bit distracted herself.

She wished she had not kept the letter from Reggie, but aside from that, now that she had heard his take on it, the letter itself worried her.

Scarecrow indeed. If Mrs. Hatfield had not written it, then who had?

Everyone else had already gone off to the pub. The last to leave—except for Laura—had been Mrs. Hatfield, who had not seemed her usual exuberant self. When Laura had asked, her friend had replied that she just felt like she might be coming down with something. Laura had reminded her about taking vitamins, and then Mrs. Hatfield had left.

Laura wiped off the last of her makeup now. That was a relief. Two more nights, and then she and Reggie would have their honeymoon back again.

Now Laura thought she heard footsteps from the stage. She called out.

"Mrs. Hatfield? Are you back?"

No answer.

Now another couple of echoing footsteps, very clear this time.

Laura called out again. No answer.

She took out her mobile phone and tried to get a connection. Nothing, not a single bar, no roaming, no wireless, nothing at all.

She stood. She knew there was no back exit from the makeup room. The only exits were at the front entrance, one on either side of the main auditorium, and then one just off the stage, behind the curtain, which led to the parking area and to the storage area for prop construction.

She couldn't reach any of them without walking either into the auditorium or onto the stage—and that's where the footsteps had come from.

Perhaps it was nothing. Perhaps Mrs. Hatfield or one of the cast members had returned and simply hadn't heard her call out. There were any number of possibilities.

But it wouldn't do just to sit and wait to find out.

She picked up the genuinely rusty steel prop sword with both hands, and she lugged it with her out onto the stage.

In front of her were the rows of audience seating, all of them in the dark.

"Hello, Mrs. Hatfield! Are you still here?"

Still no answer.

Laura began walking down the middle aisle, past the darkened rows, toward the front exit. It seemed like the best choice. The side exits both opened onto narrow, unlit areas. She was going to go right out the front, or she was going to swing the damn sword.

"Hello, everyone! Don't all answer at once!"

She had passed one dark audience row after another, and now she was more than halfway to the exit doors. And now she heard something very clearly from the rows behind her.

Applause. She turned.

In the center of one of the middle rows she had just passed, two faces were just barely visible, both of the applauders having stood. They moved into the aisle now, and Laura recognized them.

"Wonderful, dear, just wonderful! You have such a lovely speaking voice, we think you should be a professional!"

It was a nice middle-aged couple she had seen at the bar. The gentleman smiled at his wife's enthusiasm, and they both came down the aisle toward Laura.

"We hope we didn't startle you," said the man.

"We were both just so thrilled to get invited to the dress rehearsal!" said the woman.

"But . . . the dress rehearsal is over now, you know," said Laura.

"Oh," said the woman. "I'm just so clueless about these theatrical conventions. Even about the curse."

"The curse?" said Laura.

"You know, that thing where if you say the wrong word, like—"

"Shh!" said the woman's portly husband, and he quickly put his hand over her mouth for good measure.

"Excuse me," she said after she cleared her throat and he took his hand away.

Laura regarded them both curiously for a brief moment—and then there was another sound she knew well from the stage.

A board was being trodden. And at that instant, the full stage lights came on—blindingly.

She blinked, trying to focus on the figure at the middle of them.

"Welcome, Laura Penobscott!" said a male voice.

It sounded familiar. She puzzled over that, and then over a more disturbing thought: How does this person know my name?

"Yes, I know you," said the man, as if in response. "And you know me."

He stepped forward, front stage and center, and now Laura could see him clearly. He looked like the educated-sounding local from the bar, but she didn't know him.

"I do?" she said.

"You should. It is so sad when young people don't recognize their teachers. I taught you everything you know, I suspect, about world civilization."

Laura stared, and now she realized that she had been fooled by the outlandish gray hair, which had been an unruly brown back in the day. It was her social sciences teacher and dance chaperone. From twenty years ago.

"Mr. Turner!"

"Of course. I must say, you've grown up just wonderfully."

"I . . . What are you doing here?"

"I'm here for rehearsal, of course. As you are."

"Rehearsal is over."

"Oh, for the play, yes, of course. But there is still another performance scheduled for the weekend that needs work tonight."

"Mr. Turner, you aren't in the play. You don't have a role, do you?"

Mr. Turner looked surprised at that; then he smiled, and actually chuckled. Which was disconcerting; Laura have never heard anyone actually do that before.

"Does Professor Turner have a role to play?" he said. He took a couple of steps toward her, bringing him center stage, proudly, as if about to receive an award. "Does he, indeed?"

Laura presumed he was now being rhetorical. Even more worrisome—the man was referring to himself in the third person.

"Does Professor Turner have a role to play?" he said again. "Why not ask whether Professor Turner can be appointed dean of either of his departments, given his twenty years of faithful service, his many doctoral studies on the antiquities, and his own personal role in discovering the last remaining cairn grouping on Bodfyn Moor? Oh no, certainly not. We're not even certain we can find another position for Professor Turner when the school closes."

"Sorry," said Laura, trying to sound sympathetic.

"So no," he resumed. "Of course Professor Turner has no role. Certainly not in an age like this one. And certainly not here. Not in this Shakespearean thing, this play, called . . . called . . . what is the name of this play?"

"*Macbeth*?" said Laura.

The man raised his head. His eyes glimmered. His lips smiled.

"Hah! You said it!"

He pointed victoriously at Laura. She wasn't sure why.

"Excuse me?" she said.

"You said it—the word at the very top of the list of the thoughts that cannot be expressed, the images that cannot be depicted, and the words that cannot be said!"

"Oh. You mean *Macbeth*? Really?" said Laura.

"Oh no, don't pretend it doesn't matter. There are rules about what can be said, and they exist for a reason. Whether it is the curse on saying *Mac*—well, you know—or something more recent—such as carving a nonbeliever's name in a sacred stone—who are we to decide which is more valid? Such rules are what give order to society. And the more troubled the times, the more dangerous are troublesome thoughts freely expressed. Clearly you weren't paying close attention to my lectures; how you passed the tests, I'll never know. But now—we are ready to rehearse the ceremony!"

"Ceremony?" said Laura.

Mr. Turner jumped down from the stage.

Laura knew now that something was terribly wrong.

But as oddly as Mr. Turner was behaving, she was not at all afraid of him. Even at fourteen, she had been as tall as he was. She could certainly handle him now, if he was about to get out of order in some strange way.

And, of course, she had the sword. As Mr. Turner advanced toward her now, she tightened her grip on it, and got ready to raise it.

But she had forgotten about the couple behind her. They had seemed so innocent; there had been no reason to assess their capabilities.

The man, although some thirty years older than Laura, was bulky, with more muscle in his forearms than his coat revealed, and—with the advantage of surprise and the help of his lady friend—he suddenly had Laura's hands pinned behind her back.

And now Mr. Turner advanced on her with a cloth in his hand that she strongly suspected was chloroformed, but she could do nothing about it.

15

The moon was intermittent, with heavy, rapidly moving clouds concealing it one moment and then revealing it again the next.

Four figures moved fitfully across a field and away from Bodfyn. They had tried to remain out of sight on the moor, navigating through the low heath and white rocks, but now they had to risk coming back to the road just long enough to cross over the creek bridge.

What slowed their progress the most was that the bound and hooded figure was resisting, every uncertain step of the way.

"I told you we would need more help," said the portly middle-aged man.

"Shut up," said Mr. Turner. "You said you had training."

"Forty years ago, I did my two years in the army, yes," said the portly man. "But you didn't say she'd be like this. A bloody hellcat."

"I told you to watch her most recent film. That should have given you a clue."

"Please," said the portly man's wife. "We don't watch superficial action-adventure films."

There's an idea, thought Laura. So far, she'd been reacting solely by instinct. Now, it occurred to her, wasn't there some clever thing in any of the last three serial adventure films that would help her in this situation?

She ran them all quickly through memory.

No, actually, there wasn't. Unfortunately, nothing she'd been able to do in any of them lined up with her current reality. Many of the scenes—such as the ones where she was supposed to ride sidesaddle and shoot villains out of trees with a crossbow—had required stunt doubles. Laura's publicity agent was still sending hospital flowers to one of them every month.

Now they crossed the bridge. Laura felt the cobblestones under her feet and heard the water gurgling below.

And suddenly she knew exactly where she was. Mrs. Hatfield had driven them into town this way after their plane landed.

That meant that to her left must be the rising slope and the rocky tors and cairns of the moor.

And to her right must be the plane.

She stopped struggling. She tried to remember everything she could about Mr. Turner. There wasn't much. As she thought back now, it had always seemed that he stared quite a lot, but at fourteen, she had just chalked that up to his probably needing spectacles.

She remembered the ego, though. None of her teachers—and only a few people she had met since—had seemed quite so full of themselves.

Surely she could make use of that. She gave it some thought. Probably it wouldn't help just to compliment him on retaining most of his hair, but there had to be something.

Laura relaxed her arms and stopped struggling.

"Mmmmff, mmf. Mmf," she said through the gag in her mouth. She moved her head back and forth for emphasis, in the direction of Mr. Turner.

"I think she wants to say something," said the portly man.

"Mm-hmmm," said Laura, nodding. "Mm-hmmm."

"It's too late for that," said Mr. Turner.

"Not if it will stop her struggling," said the portly man. "My arms are getting tired, and every time I have to rein her in when she lurches, I can feel my sciatica acting up."

Mr. Turner stopped walking. They all did. He looked at Laura—well, at her hood at least—for a long moment.

"Do you have something you want to say to me?"

Laura nodded.

"Do you promise not to scream if I remove your gag?"

Laura nodded vigorously.

"It won't help to scream anyway, you know. We are too far out. No one will hear you."

Laura shrugged.

"All right, then," said Mr. Turner.

The portly man started to remove Laura's hood.

"No, no, not the hood," said Mr. Turner. "That will spoil the surprise. Just reach under and untie the gag."

The portly man and his wife jockeyed around a bit to get in the right position for that task. Finally, while the man held Laura's arms, his wife reached under the hood and untied the gag.

Laura gasped with relief. The sides of her mouth where the gag had pressed were as sore as if she'd been to the dentist, and she had to work her jaw back and forth, and shake off the pain, before she could speak.

"Where are you taking me?"

"Oh, I think you know."

"I don't. Really. I've tried to suss it out, but I just can't seem to get it. That's not really my fault, though, is it? You've always had a much more sophisticated intellect than I."

He nodded in agreement.

"You should try, though," he said. "Don't make excuses, young lady. Do your best. Where would I be taking you? Really now, think about it. Why should I be taking you anywhere at all?"

"For my own good?"

"Close. Try harder."

"I am trying, but it's so difficult," said Laura, and then she tried again.

"Oh, wait. I think I've got it! Of course, I should have known; it's what you've always tried to explain to people, but most of us are just too dense and caught up in our own little worlds to understand. What you are doing is for the *greater* good!"

Mr. Turner stopped walking. He looked at Laura, still with the bindings on her wrists and the hood over her face, and he let out the satisfied sigh of a man who has finally achieved a lifelong goal.

"Remove it," he said to the couple.

They both gave Mr. Turner a puzzled look.

"Are you sure?" said the portly man. "I believe the hood is to remain on. That's how I translated the runes."

"Runes?" said Laura.

Either they couldn't hear her through the cloth of the hood or they ignored her deliberately. Their discussion continued.

"This is only the rehearsal," said Mr. Turner. "Just go ahead and remove it, please."

It was an ambiguous directive. The woman thought this meant she was to loosen Laura's wrist ties, and she began to do so, with no one paying particular attention, as her husband and Mr. Turner continued to argue.

"A true rehearsal should follow the ritual precisely," said the portly man.

"Nonsense," said Mr. Turner. "If we did that all the way through, the fire would consume everything, and we'd have no one available to offer up for the event itself."

"Very well," said the portly man. "So long as we put it back on her before she is actually placed on the pyre."

He removed the hood.

"Pyre?" said Laura.

"See?" said the portly man. "I told you. Now she's going to be even more of a problem."

Mr. Turner looked at Laura, sighed, and then shook his head, as though she were a recalcitrant child.

"You're right," he said to the portly man. "And anyway, she's nowhere near as charming as I remember. Put the hood back on."

The portly man stretched the burlap sack out to its full width again and raised it up to put it over Laura's head.

As he did that, he was focused more on the hood than on Laura, and he was standing between her and Mr. Turner, which meant that at that moment, Mr. Turner didn't have a good line of sight on her, either.

Laura knew it was the best chance she would get—and she took it.

She jabbed her right elbow behind her into the portly man's solar plexus. Her range was limited by the remaining wrist ties, but still it was enough. As he gasped and bent over, she stomped the heel of her right foot backward into the instep of his wife's foot.

And then she took off running.

The only tormentor capable of immediate pursuit was Mr. Turner.

She heard him scream at her as she ran, and then, very quickly, the screams turned to cursing.

The terrain was low-scrub heath, with wild grasses that cut at bare ankles like blades, and, even more problematic, rocks.

In the intermittent moonlight, Laura could see the gray-white boulders if they were a foot or more high, just barely in time to avoid them. But smaller rocks were scattered everywhere, concealed by clumps of wild grass like deflated footballs.

She couldn't take the time to see and avoid them. She twisted her right ankle within the first dozen yards, felt the sharp pain, and had to ignore it.

She ran toward a stand of pine trees, a windbreak planted long ago, visible in dark silhouette some two hundred yards across the rocky heath. On the other side of those trees, she was certain, was the field where she and Reggie had landed their plane two nights ago.

She looked back just once, and then didn't bother again—she knew that the portly couple had now joined the pursuit—but she was sure from the sound of the cursing and bickering that she had put a little distance between herself and them.

The field grew even rockier as she approached the stand of trees. At the very edge of the stand, there were even more obstacles—not just the natural strewn rocks but also little man-made stacks of them—cairns, from centuries ago.

She got past those and into the trees. She stopped for just a moment behind a large pine, caught her breath, and got her bearings. Yes, she was in the right place. Fifty yards ahead was the break in the trees, and the green field where they had landed. Another fifty to the right should be her Cessna 150.

She heard the aggravated shouts closing in behind her, and she began her final sprint to the plane.

She saw the fixed white wings in the moonlight, the narrow blue stripe that ran along the fuselage. She guessed there might be three hundred yards of level field in front of the plane for her to take off. It was not really enough; she would not be able to get sufficient speed. But she would have to try.

She jumped in the cockpit and pressed the ignition. The engine coughed and sputtered. She saw Mr. Turner now, running toward her. She tried the ignition again, and this time the engine started.

She throttled forward in the dark. She could see silhouettes of the trees some three or four hundred yards out, but not the ground itself.

She got as much speed as she could over 100 hundred yards, 200 hundred, 250—and then she had no choice;

she was close enough to the trees now to see individual branches. She pulled back hard on the yoke.

The little Cessna went up at a sixty-degree angle, then stalled and went right back down—and that was all that Laura remembered.

16

LONDON, THE NEXT DAY

It was all one structure, all the way from the corner to midway up the block. It was a polished limestone building, modern (by London standards), with wide glass doors at the main entrance, and an engraved copper placard above them that read BAKER STREET HOUSE.

A tall fiftyish man in a worn full-length mac and carrying a violin case walked up to the entrance. He knew this was the right place, but he was delayed when he got to the doors, because tourists, mostly American and Japanese, were milling about in front of him, with puzzled expressions and mobile phone cameras at the ready, walking back and forth between these doors and the door of the next establishment up the block.

As the tall man began to open one of the heavy glass doors, one of the American tourists turned toward him.

"Is this where—"

"No."

"But the next door up is the Beatles store at 233 Baker Street, and there are no other address numbers between here and the beginning of the block. So this must be where—"

"It isn't, he doesn't, and he'd be long since dead even if he ever did. Excuse me, please."

"But—"

"Please, you are blocking the door," said the tall man as he finally pushed through and into the wide marble-floored lobby.

He shook his head, annoyed with himself. He should not have been rude. He especially, because he, more than most people, fully understood.

But he hadn't much time.

In the lobby, the employees of Dorset Bank, which had offices on the main floor, were arriving at work in proper business attire, walking back and forth with cups of cappuccino from the sandwich shop across the street.

One of them gave the tall man a sideways look, followed by a glance at the security guard to get the guard's attention.

The tall man didn't mind. If he had seen a man in a full raincoat and carrying a worn black musician's case containing God knows what, he would have said something, too. Especially having been a bank teller at one time himself.

The security guard, a white-haired man, elderly but in seemingly excellent physical condition for his age, was seated at the security desk at the center of the lobby. From the way he was blinking and putting his glasses on and off, it was obvious that his eyesight was not the best. The tall man helpfully went directly up to him.

"Good morning, Hendricks," he said.

"Ah, good morning, sir," said the security guard. He took his glasses off now and began to clean the lenses. "Haven't seen you here in quite a while."

"Hasn't been necessary in quite a while," said the tall man.

"I'm afraid none of the leasing committee is in at the moment," said the guard. "Or the board of directors, either. Although Mr. Rafferty is expected back soon."

"That's all right. Today I'll just pay a visit to the second floor."

"Very good, sir."

The tall man went to the lift. The directory there listed only one name for the second floor. It was for a sublet tenant—something calling itself Baker Street Chambers.

The tall man got in the lift and pressed the button for that floor.

On the second floor, a fiftyish woman, short in height and comfortably plump in the English way, dressed in pleasant shades of business gray and pastel apricot, sat behind the receptionist's desk with her head in her hands.

On her desk was a stack of incoming letters and an opened laptop.

She raised her head to look at the photo image that was displayed on the laptop, but just as every time before, the worry came back, her lungs tightened, and her head sank in her hands again.

Now, mercifully, her phone rang. She picked up immediately.

"Nigel, it's about time!" she said. "Why haven't we heard from them?"

"Can you speak up a bit?" said the voice at the other end. "It's not a great connection, and I'm on the Ventura Freeway."

"I said, I haven't heard anything from them at all!"

"I shouldn't worry if I were you," said the voice through the phone. "Although if I were me, I would, and I will when I get back, given that all of Reggie's disgruntled clients find a way of letting me know that they regard me as a poor second choice."

"It's me they complain to first," said Lois. "The barrister's clerk always takes the heat before anyone else. But that's not why you should be worried. You should be worried because he's your brother, she's your new sister-in-law, and you have no idea where they are. Or so you say."

"I don't," said Nigel. "And that's the way they wanted

it. They are on their honeymoon, for God's sake, and if they have the energy to keep it going, who am I to track them down and interrupt? I expect we'll hear from them when they're good and ready to return, like adolescent cats."

"But they're not adolescent cats. They are grown-ups. And grown-ups of whatever species should not just vanish without telling responsible people where they are going!"

Lois paused for him to say something reassuring.

She had to wait several moments, partly because the connection was so bad that it was hard for Nigel to pick up on her tone of voice, and also because he was indeed on the freeway; he heard horns and squealing brakes and realized he had just nearly caused a pileup of all the vehicles behind him, and he had to pull over.

"Do you think we should call the police?" asked Lois, still waiting for his response.

"And tell them two grown-ups are on their honeymoon and haven't checked in?"

"Yes."

Now, given a moment, Nigel thought about it and understood: Lois believed the reason Reggie and Laura hadn't shared their destination—and had, in her opinion, gone missing—was because of that one mistake she had made with the paparazzi.

His sigh was audible, despite the bad connection.

"Lois, they are most certainly fine, and it is not your fault that they've gone into hiding. As you said, they're grown-ups. Or at least one of them is, and as long as my brother, Reggie, does what Laura says, one is enough."

Perhaps that made sense, although Lois wasn't sure. But now the phone connection grew even weaker, she thought she heard something like horns honking again, and in another moment Nigel declared something about not being able to talk, and the connection went dead.

Lois sighed. Despite Nigel's attempt at dispensation—if that's what it was—she was still certain that it was all her fault.

She couldn't get that out of her head, sitting alone at her desk at Baker Street Chambers. Everything in chambers had been put on hold, because everyone in the legal community knew there was no barrister present. Not the senior barrister, Reggie Heath, QC, and not even the junior barrister, Nigel Heath, with his new license. He had gotten an invitation from his overseas girlfriend to come back and try his luck with her again—hence his presence in Los Angeles. So no one was present now except the receptionist, the chambers clerk, and the secretary.

That is to say, it was just Lois, by herself.

And then on top of it all, there were all those incoming letters. They were another matter entirely.

There were times when she wished simply that the man himself were real. That the person to whom the letters were addressed actually existed. Then they would be his problem.

But of course he wasn't real; he was fictional. Only the

letters were real, and they were on Lois's desk, and so Lois had another real problem, in addition to the one she was actually worried about. She sighed and closed her eyes, wishing the bloody things would just go away.

But her wish was interrupted. She couldn't even have the satisfaction of imagining it, because now a little bell chimed, alerting her that the lift had brought someone up.

The doors opened. A tall man carrying a violin case stepped out of the lift onto the hardwood floor and paused to get his office bearings.

He was rather unkempt. And he did not have the look of the chambers' usual visitors, who were typically solicitors in somber brown suits, looking for a barrister to represent their clients. If anything, this man must be one of the clients. He surely wasn't a solicitor.

But Lois was no snob, and was disinclined to act on presuppositions, and she smiled pleasantly as he stepped up to her desk.

"How can I help you?" asked Lois.

"I gather business is not exactly humming," said the man. "At least not the paying business."

"Why do you say that?"

"It's obvious. Law chambers that have only one person—you—as receptionist, barrister's clerk, and secretary cannot be doing terribly well."

"I didn't ask how you came to the conclusion," said Lois. "I asked why you said it. I mean, it's an odd way of requesting a barrister's assistance."

"I'm not requesting a barrister's assistance," said the tall man. "At least not in a barrister's capacity."

Lois puzzled over that for a moment, and she studied the man closely.

"You look familiar," said Lois.

"Yes," said the tall man. "I suppose I do."

"I've seen you in the underground. You're a busker. You play the violin for tips."

"Yes," he said. "I've been many things. I believe you tossed in a tenner once. I appreciated it."

"It was rather an accident," said Lois. "I was searching for something smaller, and when I realized it was all I had, I was too embarrassed to toss in nothing at all."

"I appreciated it, either way."

She studied him a moment longer.

"Do you . . . make much of a living doing that?"

"Not as bad as you might think. The tips are good in the city. Not enough to keep a flat in London, of course."

"Where do you live, then?"

He just raised an eyebrow, then shrugged.

"Do you have a name?"

"My friends call me Sig."

"Unusual. Short for Sigmund?"

"What else would it be short for?"

"Oh, I don't know, but I think there are some Scandinavian surnames that begin with *Sig*—"

"Well, it's not important," said the man quickly. "Sig, or Siger, either short form is fine. In any case, I can see that your employer is not here. He is on his honeymoon, I surmise."

"What makes you say that?"

"Are you asking how I reached the conclusion this time, or why I bothered pointing it out?"

"This time, I'm asking both."

"Very well. First, there is the stack of incoming correspondence on your desk. I can tell from your attire that you are an efficient person who takes her responsibilities seriously. Surely you would not have so many unprocessed letters on your desk if the person to whom they were addressed were here to receive them."

"Ha!" said Lois. "You've got it wrong."

"I have? You mean your employer is here after all?"

"Um, no. I just mean that the person to whom they are addressed is not my employer and is never here to receive them."

"Oh? Why is that?"

"None of your business."

"My apologies. But in any case, the stack of letters tells me that your employer is not here, and the photo on your laptop tells me why. No, no, you needn't power down now to hide it; I've already seen it. It is a wedding photo. Somewhat more disorderly than most, I must say. You are in the photo, the maid of honor, apparently. The groom— that tall fellow with the air of someone who thinks he knows everything—is most certainly a barrister. He must be the head of these chambers. I suppose one could attribute his expression just to his incredible luck at snagging that redheaded beauty standing next to him, but the confidence of his expression indicates that he's had this smugness for some time; therefore, he is the QC for these chambers. His younger brother is a junior barrister in these chambers, which is not a guess, actually, because I believe I met him once on jury duty. In any case, there you are, in the photo, looking quite alarmed and as though you are about to throw a bouquet of flowers at someone, and not in the traditionally good way. Do I have any of it right?"

"I confirm or deny nothing, because it's none of your business. But I'll allow you to believe what you like."

"You are very kind," said Siger. "I would also point out some items in the background of the photo that make me think the location for the vows was rather hastily arranged. But I am not here regarding your employer's family issues. I am here because it has come to my attention that your employer appears to be neglecting his duty regarding these—"

Siger put his hand firmly on the stack of letters on Lois's desk.

"When you say 'these,' what, exactly, is it that you think—"

The man shook his head dismissively and picked up a handful of the letters. He read their addresses in rapid succession.

"'To Mr. Sherlock Holmes, at 221B Baker Street.' And

'To Mr. Sherlock Holmes, Consulting Detective, at 221B Baker Street.' And 'To Mr. Sherlock Holmes and Dr. John Watson, at 221B Baker Street.' Shall I go on?"

"Um . . . what, exactly, is your point?"

Siger sighed, then said, "It is common knowledge, you know. The original banking establishment that put up this building in the 1930s, when the two hundred block of Baker Street was first created—well, the moment they opened the doors, the Royal Mail began delivering the letters here, and from then on, the owners of this building have always faithfully fulfilled their duties in caring for them. Your employer—the Baker Street Law Chambers—for whom you clerk, only began to receive the letters in the last few years, when your senior QC took the sublet of this floor. And I'm sure he could only do so under the express condition that he take responsibility for responding to the letters addressed to Sherlock Holmes."

"Yes, yes, that is all true," said Lois. "But Reggie Heath, QC, and his brother are both away. So I don't think there is anyone here to help you. Whatever it is that you want."

Siger smiled kindly and, unbidden, sat down in the guest chair by her desk.

"Forgive me, dear woman, but whether it is business of mine or not is beside the point. The point is that the letters are going unanswered. That must not be."

Now he reached for a letter from the incoming baskets, but he got one from the wrong stack.

Lois told him so.

"No, those are already done," she said. "Or at least opened. That's the stack that Nigel finished before all bloody hell broke loose."

"Oh?"

He unfolded the letter and glanced at it very briefly, but Lois didn't give him time to read it.

"That is, before I bolluxed up the entire wedding plan at the rehearsal," she said.

"Ah," said Sig. He put the letter down and looked again at the photo on her laptop. "Of course. All bloody hell. The wedding."

"Yes. Because I bolluxed everything up. Now Nigel has gone back to America to try to patch things up with his girlfriend, Mara—or else he is just driving aimlessly around on the motorways I think, from the sound of it. But the letters are piling up, and Reggie and Laura are missing, and it's all my fault!"

"Hmm," said Siger. He sat back in his chair, closed his eyes, and pressed his fingertips together in the shape of a gable roof, perfectly pitched on both sides. When he was fully settled, and balanced, apparently, he said, "Tell me everything that happened. Start from the beginning. Don't leave anything out, no matter how insignificant it might seem."

"Oh, please," said Lois, and she gave him a glare to make sure he caught her attitude.

But he didn't move. His eyes remained closed.

And though she hadn't really intended to, something in the man's pose made Lois willing to talk. In any case, she had to talk to someone; she was about to burst if she didn't.

"If only I hadn't got tipsy on the Chianti," she began, sighing deeply. "Then I know I wouldn't have sat down next to Nigel and Mara and said, 'So, my dears, when are you two going to follow suit and tie the knot yourselves?'"

She glanced at Siger, fully expecting to see a judgmental reaction from him, but there was nothing. She continued.

"One should never say that at a wedding, of course. And here I had gone and done it. And then—oh, and then when I saw the faces of the two dears—well, one of them anyway, because Nigel's reaction was quite the opposite of Mara's, and that became the problem—I knew I had put my foot in it, and well above the ankle, too.

"Mara was on a plane back to America the next day. It took hours of prying to get Nigel to admit it, but I knew: It was she who had blanched, not him.

"But that wasn't the worst of it. Oh no, the worst was what I did to the Laura Rankin/Reggie Heath wedding plans themselves."

Again she checked for Siger's reaction, and still he showed nothing.

"The location of the wedding had to be a secret," she continued, "because the paparazzi simply wouldn't let Laura alone."

"Mmm-hmm," said Siger without moving a muscle.

"They had scouts out just everywhere trying to figure out where it would be. So we had a wedding rehearsal in advance at a different location in London, at Hampstead Heath, to divert them from where the actual wedding would be in Cornwall. We had a little dinner party after the rehearsal in Hampstead Heath. We knew paparazzi spies would try to weasel in among Laura's celebrity friends, and that was the whole point, to let them think they had found the actual location, when, in fact, it was going to be somewhere else. All it required was that we be alert and very careful about everything we said."

Lois stopped, a catch in her voice.

"And I am normally a very discreet person!" she said.

"Focus, please," said the man, his eyes still closed.

"It was my fourth glass of wine that did it. That and the Italian gentleman who offered it to me. But he was wearing such a very respectable gray suit, and he had spoken so knowledgeably about gardening and how to prune roses, that it just did not occur to me that he was the paparazzi spy. I thought he was Nigel's girlfriend's cousin. And when he got me talking about the flowers that would be at the wedding, and whether they would be locally grown or brought in, and I started to brag about the roses that Laura's aunt grows at her estate in Cornwall—well, I know that's what did it. That's how the paparazzi knew how to find the actual wedding, and spring out from behind those very rosebushes at the last minute, with their nasty cameras flashing and clicking away, and pursuing Reggie and Laura across the lawn. I managed to delay two of them by tipping a reception centerpiece into their path—it was one of those bubbling chocolate things that you dip strawberries into. But it helped for only a moment. There was barely time for Mr. Spenser—that's Laura's aunt's butler—to take Reggie and Laura in the groundskeeper's lawn tractor out past the back lawns, where Laura's aunt keeps their old Cessna 150 covered up in a shed. I had no idea anyone in her family even knew how to fly. Laura got in the pilot's seat and Reggie in the passenger's, and Spenser cleared the stored antique furniture and bric-a-brac out of their way, and off they went."

Lois stopped for a breath. And now she began to tear up from the reliving of it.

"And—and—now we haven't heard a word from Reggie and Laura, and that plane looked to me like it's older than I am, and God knows what might have happened to them!"

Siger's eyelids fluttered, and then one opened completely.

"Please don't cry," he said.

"Sorry," said Lois, sniffling.

Siger stood, found a box of tissues on Lois's desk and handed it to her. Then he picked up the opened envelope and letter that he had handled a moment earlier. He gave them both to Lois.

"Notice that the envelope has postage, but it was never canceled," he said. "There is a date and time stamp, but not one from the Royal Mail—just the one that the mail room of this building uses to mark the arrival of incoming mail."

Lois looked at it.

"This was received on the day Reggie and Laura left for the wedding in Cornwall," she said.

"Was the younger brother, Nigel, still here in chambers at that time?"

"No. He had gone to the States to try to get his girlfriend back. He even missed the wedding itself."

"Does the older brother ever open and read these letters?"

"No, hardly ever, if he can help it. Especially not when he was trying to wrap up work and get away on his honeymoon."

"Then who opened this one?"

"I know it wasn't me," said Lois. "I don't refold the letters and tuck them back in the envelopes like that."

"Then who could it have been?"

"Why . . . it would have to have been Laura! She must have sat here at my desk to wait for Reggie!"

"Yes," said Siger, nodding slightly. "I think I detect just the slightest scent of transferred perfume on it that would have been hers—she would have had to hold it for several minutes for that to occur. And I think it puts things in perspective. It's quite a nice little problem."

"Is it?" said Lois. "Nigel seems to think I'm worried over nothing."

"Perhaps," said Siger. "But read the letter."

Lois did so, aloud:

> "Dear Mr. Sherlock Holmes:
>
> I swore a solemn vow not to tell a single living soul. But it is said that you are a character of fiction. And therefore not a living soul. I can tell you, then, without breaking my vow:
>
> Something is terribly wrong in Bodfyn. Please send Scarecrow."

"And no signature," said Lois when she finished reading.

"No," said Siger. "And the 'scarecrow' reference is puzzling. Have you any idea what it means?"

"No."

"Do you know what the letter might mean to Laura Rankin? That she would hold on to it and study it for so long, and then make a photocopy of it to take with her on her own honeymoon?" asked Siger.

"No. What makes you think she made a copy of it?"

"Some people carry their coffee cups with them to the copy machine," said Siger. "And sometimes they—probably Nigel, because you would be too careful—spill a bit on the underside of the top cover, and the coffee spill dries, and when the next poor soul comes along to use it—that would have been Laura, the following day or so—they get a faint coffee-stain mark on the back of whatever original they are copying."

"Oh," said Lois. "Well, I'm sure you are right about all that. I'll just go get a paper towel and clean that thing—"

"Please," said Siger. "The coffee stain will keep. Now, if it were only the letter, I would see a puzzle, but no cause for concern. If it were only Laura and Reggie's being so late, I would see reason for some mild concern, but no real puzzle to investigate. But given both—well, that's too much of a coincidence. And finally, there's you. You are too worried to let it go. And so we won't. I don't believe we should wait. The aunt's home is on the Cornwall coast, is it not? Do you drive, by the way? I did once—I was even a cabbie for a while—but that was decades ago, I'm more than a bit rusty, and my license is quite expired."

Lois stared at the man in astonishment.

"Whatever are you saying? Do you really think I would just get up and go with a strange man I have never met on a trip with no one else, and—"

"I understand your concerns, and I try not to seem strange, but I was hoping you would make an exception."

"What I will do is call Mr. Hendricks," said Lois, reaching for the phone. "And don't you underestimate him; he's quite capable of coming up here and—"

"I don't doubt it for a minute. And of course I spoke to

him already before I came up. But perhaps it would help if I provide a personal recommendation?"

"From whom?"

"One moment, please."

Siger took a mobile phone out of his coat pocket— somewhat to Lois's surprise—and sent a text. Then he put the phone back in his pocket and said, "If he is in, this should only take a moment."

Lois just stared at Siger for a moment and said nothing. Siger said nothing, either, just watched the lights on the lift, which showed that someone was coming down from the top floor.

Now the lift chimed and the doors opened. Mr. Rafferty stepped out. He saw Siger, showed recognition more than surprise, and then turned to Lois.

"Hello, Lois."

"Mr. Rafferty—do you know this man?"

"Yes. I've known him for quite a few years."

"Is he . . . is he . . . well, sane?"

"I believe so."

"Do you think it is . . . safe . . . for me to travel to Cornwall with him?"

Rafferty considered carefully before answering. Finally, he said, "Lois, I can assure you that whatever Mr. Siger's intentions are, they are strictly honorable. Although I cannot speak to his merits as a traveling companion, I can say confidently that you have nothing to fear from him. You must follow your own instincts, of course. But—"

"But what?"

"But I can also tell you this: If you do not accompany him, I believe the continued residence of the Baker Street Chambers at this address may well be in jeopardy."

17

It was a five-hour drive, according to the travel apps, from London to Newquay, in Cornwall, but Lois managed it in just over four. If Siger was terrified along the way, he concealed it well—for most of the drive at least.

Aunt Mabel's estate, known to the registries as Darby House, had been built in the seventeenth century, a genuine castle with turrets of yellow-gray stone. It was highly civilized now, with indoor plumbing on all floors, though it wasn't always functioning properly. Lawns and low garden hedges extended hundreds of yards in all directions.

The estate was protected by a manned security gate off the main road. As Lois and Siger drove up, the guard came out with his clipboard. He saw Lois, recognized her immediately, made a face that seemed rather like a grimace, and opened the gate.

Before they drove in, Lois rolled the window down and spoke to the guard as though he would know exactly what she was talking about.

"Once again, let me just say that I am so very, very sorry."

The guard said nothing and waved them in.

"Hmm," said Siger as they drove in.

"What?" said Lois.

"The paving on this driveway is pristine, but in front of the gate, I saw metal and rubber scuff marks of the kind made when someone changes a tire. And the security guard has minor scrapes on his knuckles, indicating that he was the one doing the work, even though the only transportation of his own nearby is a golf cart. So, given your profuse apology just now, I surmise that the paparazzi used the old 'We have a flat tire; won't you help us?' ploy to distract the guard and get in the gate."

"Yes," said Lois as they drove onto the roundabout in front of the house. "Pretty much. So kind of you to bring it up."

"I believe it was you who brought it up at the gate," replied Siger.

Now they were in front of Darby House. The heavy oaken door opened, and a butler came down the steps to greet them.

He introduced himself as Spenser. He looked to be as old as the sycamores that shielded the estate from the main road, but he was not nearly so tall. He had a comb-over of his balding pate that was so obvious, it screamed defiance—it knew it was an obvious comb-over, and it didn't care.

"Lady Darby will be so . . . pleased . . . to see you," said the butler to Lois, not trying to disguise his doubt very much. "And your . . . friend."

"Oh, he's not my friend," said Lois quickly. "I mean, not like that Italian fellow I brought from the wedding rehearsal. . . . I mean, he's not a paparazzo; I'm quite sure of it. He's just . . . a fellow who came up from the tube station this morning, and he . . . well, never mind, I'm sure that's not important. Anyway, I just want to say that I am just so very, very sorry about everything that happened."

Spenser said nothing in response to that, apparently pretending that no explanation was necessary, and he proceeded to escort Lois and Siger through the main level of Darby House.

"Hmm," said Siger as they followed Spenser.

"What now?" asked Lois.

"Nothing," said Siger.

"Go ahead, say it."

"I noticed a second golf cart parked at the edge of the front lawn. An estate of this size must have a groundskeeper, who would have a small domestic tractor/mower for doing his work. This golf cart, though, is for the butler, so he can get around quickly and supervise things."

"And? Don't stop now."

"I noticed two different kinds of mud on the wheels, and even a bit on the running board of the cart. Some of it matches that in the front garden, where there have recently been some hasty repairs. But there's also a grayish, less domesticated bit of earth that would have had to come from the uncultivated area adjacent to the estate lawn. And on one of the doors I saw a brown substance that I'm sure isn't mud at all, but something like—"

"Yes?"

"Melted chocolate, I would guess, without tasting it. Also there are traces of a whitish substance—cake frosting. Probably buttercream. So, given all those facts and your profuse apology to the butler, I would venture that the paparazzi attacked not only by car through the gate but also on foot, sneaking through the gardens, and even tromping across from the moors. Someone—I presume Mr. Spenser here—jumped in his cart to try to corral them after they had breached the estate, but he had limited success. They must have penetrated all the way into the reception itself, and in a desperate attempt to deter them, someone—you, Lois, I presume—not only tried to tip the chocolate fountain into their path but also attacked them with the wedding cake, and Spenser drove through it all as he pursued the knaves in his cart. Do I have it right?"

Siger addressed the question to Lois, but it was the butler who answered.

"Not all of it, sir," observed Spenser matter-of-factly.

"You missed the part where they scaled the cliffs from the beach and came at us across the back lawn."

"Yes," said Siger. "I imagined they might, but I wanted to see the back lawn before offering an opinion."

Lois stopped walking now.

"Something wrong?" asked Siger.

"Yes," said Lois. "Would you please stop enumerating all the disasters that I caused?"

"I will if you will," said Siger.

Now they continued on to the back of the house. Spenser opened the doors to a terrace overlooking the back lawn—or park, really, from the size of it. The garden hedge to the south was at least a quarter mile away, and whatever boundary there was for the lawn to the east was completely out of sight, beyond a gentle uphill slope.

Two hundred yards or so to the west were the cliffs and the Atlantic Ocean.

On the terrace, the scene was quite tranquil at the moment. Aunt Mabel was already there, having tea and scones and lemon marmalade, and a morning newspaper lay on the table. The green lawns of Darby House stretched out in the distance.

Spenser announced Lois and Siger to Aunt Mabel and then went away.

Aunt Mabel was in her seventies, tall, with a leisurely pace in her speech that conveyed that at this stage of her life, with all that she had already seen, she could no longer be ruffled.

She looked up, saw Lois, controlled any sign of alarm, smiled slightly, and cleared her throat.

"Do sit down, both of you. So good of you to drop by. Spenser will be back with fresh tea in just a moment."

Siger was staring out toward the cliffs.

"They had a rather short runway, didn't they?" he said as he sat down. "I can see the impressions of the plane's wheels in the grass from here. You keep the plane in the barn by that stand of sycamores. Under normal circumstances, it would be pushed out from the barn fifty yards or so, and then get up to speed on that nice long field to the east, but they were in a hurry. I gather they started the plane while still in the barn, and came straight out and—well—straight over the cliff."

Aunt Mabel ignored that long enough to take care of more important business.

"There's sugar, milk, and lemon," she said to Siger, because he didn't seem to be paying attention to them. "You may take your choice, as I'm sure you won't want them all in one."

Now she looked out toward the cliffs and sighed.

"Yes, I'll admit my heart was in my throat for the brief moment in which they dropped out of sight, but then we heard the engine at full throttle, and up they came. They flew out over the water first, and then turned around and went off to the east, and before we lost sight of them, Laura waggled the plane's beautiful turquoise wings for us, in celebration of their escape."

Aunt Mabel allowed herself a little self-satisfied smile, then said, "One of the paparazzi was so busy with his camera that he almost fell over the cliff himself. Such a shame that he didn't."

"But you haven't heard a word from them since?" asked Lois.

"No, dear," said Aunt Mabel. "But I'm sure they're fine. Laura is an excellent pilot. The last time she took the plane out, she handled it just brilliantly. I remember it very well; it was to celebrate her . . . twenty-first birthday. . . ."

Aunt Mabel's voice trailed off as they all did the math and realized how long it had been since Laura had flown.

"Well," said Aunt Mabel finally. "Where is Spenser with that tea? Have either of you seen the morning paper yet?"

She picked it up from the table and began to unfold it.

"I find these days that there are some headlines that I'm willing to read, and others that I just can't bear to—"

She stopped mid-sentence, staring at the paper. For a moment, she didn't breathe.

Then she laid the paper down on the table, and with great effort, she held her composure and remained very still.

Lois reached for the paper. Siger watched Aunt Mabel's eyes as Lois read the heading and first few lines aloud, Aunt Mabel showing a glimmer of hope that somehow it would be different when Lois read it. And then the glimmer vanished when the words were the same.

Early that morning, the wreckage of a small plane had been discovered in the national forest preserve near Bodfyn. It was a vintage Cessna 150 with turquoise wings.

"The . . . victims have not been identified," said Lois. "And neither has the serial number of the plane. It says that right here."

"Yes," said Siger informatively, "often in such instances bodies are burned beyond recognition."

Lois gave Siger a look, then said, "There can be many old planes with wings of a particular color. I mean, it doesn't say that here, but it's what I think."

Lois said that for Aunt Mabel's benefit, but Lois herself was holding it together only with effort.

"Bodfyn is to the north," said Siger. "But you said they deliberately turned and went east. That's the wrong direction for where this plane was found."

Lois couldn't tell whether Siger was trying to be better at consolation now, or just picky about the facts.

Aunt Mabel nodded in response.

"Yes," she said quite softly. "But they could have done that just to throw the paparazzi off."

"Well, I'm sure they wouldn't be heading toward this place called Bodfyn anyway," said Lois, consolingly. "Who goes there?"

"Laura went to school near there, in the year or so between when her parents died and when I brought her to live with me," said Aunt Mabel.

"So you think she had fond memories and wanted to go back?" asked Siger.

"I wouldn't say that, exactly. It's not where I would have sent them on their honeymoon, God knows. There's just nothing there, it is so out of the way. But perhaps that would be the point—to get away to a place where tourists and paparazzi never go?"

The more they talked, the more worried Aunt Mabel had become, and now she stood suddenly, on the verge of tears.

"I'll have to go there," said Aunt Mabel. "I'll have Spenser bring the car around. You are both welcome to stay here, if you like, and—and—"

Aunt Mabel steadied herself on the table for just an instant, and then her entire tall frame just seemed to collapse.

Siger was up in an instant to catch her before she hit the ground.

18

Laura's aunt Mabel was sitting up and drinking tea once more. The doctor had been summoned when she fainted, and Lois and Siger had remained to be sure she was all right.

But Spenser was there in any case, and he had the situation well in hand—rather aggressively in hand, in fact, not allowing Lois and Siger to do much of anything, and actively encouraging them to be on their way.

Lois tried to reassure Aunt Mabel before leaving.

"You mustn't worry about a thing," she said. "I'm sure all is fine. It most surely was not Laura and Reggie's plane, just one that resembled it. No one can ever agree on what turquoise looks like anyway, and there are many small planes with blue wings. I'm so certain of it that we will go there ourselves to be sure. Won't we, Mr. Siger?"

"Yes," he said. "We will."

Aunt Mabel half-raised herself out of her chair and said, "Lois, dear, please just be very, very careful in whatever you do."

Lois wasn't sure whether that remark was regarding their safety or about not bolluxing things up. She decided not to ask for clarification.

Aunt Mabel sat back down, sipped her tea, and directed Spenser to help them to their rental car.

Spenser nearly slammed the door on Siger's fingertips as he wished them (or so he said) Godspeed.

They got under way, heading out on the long estate drive, past the green lawns, and onto the main road.

Siger turned to Lois and said, "That was clever of you, using Aunt Mabel's distress as an excuse for us to go to the site."

"What excuse?" said Lois. "That is why we're going, isn't it?"

"Oh. Yes, of course," said Siger.

It was dusk now, after nearly two hours on the road.

Lois drove, because Siger said he hadn't done so in more than twenty years. She was trying to fight back tears. It was just as well that she was doing the driving, she thought, because if she had not been, she would have given in to them altogether, and surely that would help no one. Perhaps herself, but it was no time to be selfish.

Siger, in the passenger seat, amused himself for a while with Lois's smart phone. Then he put it away, and for the remainder of the drive just sat with his eyes closed and his hands folded over his diaphragm, fingers interlocked. He was silent, but Lois didn't think he was asleep, because the tips of his thumbs were now pressed together, as his fingertips had been when he sat in the chambers at Baker Street.

After nearly two hours on the road, they reached the turnoff for the village of Amesbury. Lois slowed for the turn, and Siger opened his eyes.

"What are you doing?" he asked.

"Taking the turn to Amesbury."

Siger shook his head.

"There's no point," he said. "The coroner's office is only open to the public until five, and it's past that, so if he is in town, we won't get to see him until tomorrow anyway. But if he's doing his job properly, he isn't even there. He should still be at the crash site with the air investigations team, and that's a few miles up ahead."

Lois brought the car to a stop on the side of the road. She didn't say anything; she wouldn't even look at him.

It took Siger a moment, but finally he saw a tear running down her left cheek, and he understood.

"If you feel unable to view the crash site," he said, "we won't go there. At least not tonight. I reserved two rooms in Amesbury. We can spend the night there and wait until the coroner's office opens in the morning."

Lois considered it, then shook her head.

"No," she said. "Aunt Mabel deserves to know, one

way or the other, as soon as possible. I owe them that much. If you think the coroner will be at the crash site, then we will go there now."

"Another ten minutes down the road, then," said Siger. "Although I disagree about what you owe."

Lois said nothing to that, and she pulled out onto the road.

With the last sense of the sun faded, and no lamps at all on the country road, it was near pitch-black. Lois put the high beams on, but their trajectory in the rental car was poorly adjusted—she could see in the distance at an angle, or up close straight ahead, but she could not do both at the same time. She switched back and forth anxiously between them, certain that she would miss the turn.

"It will be in a quarter mile on your left," said Siger without opening his eyes. "About thirty seconds. You've done an excellent job of maintaining a steady speed, so I think my calculations will prove correct."

Lois slowed and switched to the low beams. There it was. The turn was unmarked; they might well have missed it.

They drove under a canopy of old oak trees, on a road that was barely wide enough for a single vehicle. With only intermittent moonlight between the clouds, they continued on for several minutes through open fields, then across a stone bridge that traversed a creek, and finally up a gradual slope to the top of a hill.

As she slowed at the top of the hill, Lois could see bright

white lights on the other side, and she knew what they must mean. She stopped the car. Siger opened his eyes.

Lois got out of the car, and a moment later, so did Siger.

They both stood and looked, without saying a word.

The road led down the hill and into a meadow. The meadow was bordered on the opposite side of the valley by a stand of tall pines, in dark silhouette against the sky. To the right, farther north, was the glimmer of a distant lake.

But what Lois cared about was just a few hundred yards down the slope from where they were standing. She had never seen plane wreckage before, except on the telly, and that, of course, was just from the point of view of the person holding the camera.

She hadn't known what to expect, nor wanted to think about it, but what struck her now, looking down the slope toward the site, was how mundane the actual plane seemed, compared to the activity going on around it.

There was no field of strewn debris. The little plane had apparently just gone nose-down into the ground. Lois had no idea what might have caused that and was not inclined to guess. All she knew for certain was that the propeller and cab of the plane were bent and broken in front of the trees, the fuselage sticking into the air at almost a ninety-degree angle, and the wings intact.

None of that mattered. What distressed her was that, even from here, she could see that the plane had been fully engulfed in flame.

She could see the blackened metal and other materials clearly, because the entire scene, for a radius of about fifty yards out from the plane, was bathed in the bright white of floodlamps. Behind a perimeter of orange tape, Air Accident inspectors in fluorescent yellow vests hovered around the burned wreckage of the plane.

"We should go down there now," said Siger. "There may still be something to be learned. Please do not be concerned that you will see—"

He stopped.

"See what?" said Lois.

Siger cleared his throat, then said, "The bodies will have already been removed."

Lois made no response to that. She got back in the driver's seat, started the engine without saying another word, and put the car in motion before Siger could even close his door.

They drove to within twenty yards of the perimeter and stopped. A small crowd of spectators had come from somewhere and gathered around in the dark—a loose cluster of civilians, standing outside the perimeter tape, staring in, talking among themselves in hushed voices, and maneuvering for better views of the burnt wreckage.

Several cars were parked nearby as well, just outside the range of the lamps.

"Is it a tourist attraction, then?" asked Lois.

"Locals, I think," said Siger. "I noticed the tire tracks

in the mud when we made our turn. These people came in the smaller passenger sedans from the opposite direction on the main road. There's a smaller village out that way, too small, probably, for its own full emergency services. The larger vehicles—the initial emergency responders as well as the investigators who arrived in those two white vans—came from the same direction we did."

"So the locals don't have anything better to do in the evening?" said Lois, as she got out of the car.

Siger didn't respond; he was already walking toward the perimeter tape, where a man sporting a red handlebar mustache was coming away from the scene. The man wore a white lab coat, walked with authority, and held up his hand when he saw them . . .

"Stay behind the tape," he said.

"You are the coroner, I presume?" said Siger.

"I have no comments for the press," said the man.

"Goodness. I hope we don't look like we are from the tabloids," said Lois, stepping up to the perimeter with Siger.

"I can see that you aren't locals," said the coroner. "And if you aren't reporters, you can keep an even further distance. I have no patience with vulture tourism."

"My friend here believes she might be next of kin," said Siger, lying.

Lois started to gasp, but she stifled it.

"That's interesting. Next of kin to whom? I've made no identification yet," said the coroner.

"To put a finer point on it, she represents the only surviving family member of Laura Rankin."

The coroner considered that for a moment. He sniffled, and rubbed his mustache with his fingers. Then he cleared his throat—painfully, by the sound of it.

"Would you like a lozenge?" said Lois, quite sincerely.

The coroner regarded them both suspiciously.

"If you have legitimate questions regarding identification of the remains, you may go to my office in Amesbury tomorrow morning at eight."

"Thank you," said Siger.

Now the coroner turned abruptly away, distracted by a tweedy pensioner couple who were too close to the perimeter tape.

"You there! Stay behind it, please," he yelled, his voice cracking.

He turned back to Lois.

"You offered a lozenge?"

Lois produced one from a pack in her purse. The coroner thanked her, then turned away again and went back to his work.

Lois turned to Siger.

"He didn't say it was them," she said. "I don't think he said that."

"No," said Siger. "He very carefully said nothing. Which is quite the correct response until he knows."

There were both standing apart from the other civilians, but now someone called out to them.

"Hello there!"

It was the gentleman in the tweed coat and his wife, who a moment earlier had had their knuckles rapped for intruding a bit too close on the perimeter. The woman looked a bit sheepish about it. The gentleman came striding toward Lois and Siger now with a friendly smile.

"I don't believe we've met before, have we?" said the man, extending his hand. "We've been in the village more than a week now, and thought we'd seen everyone there is to see!"

Siger politely shook the man's hand.

"My name is Siger. My . . . colleague, Lois."

The couple introduced themselves as Nancy and Roy. They were staying at someone's little house in a village named Bodfyn, which they felt very lucky to have arranged through Airbnb, because the village had no hotels.

"And what about you two?" Nancy continued. "Do you have a place to stay?"

"We're in Amesbury," said Lois. "We only drove out to pay a visit to the—"

Siger interrupted.

"A visit to Bodfyn," he said quickly. "We're only staying in Amesbury because, as you say, the accommodations in Bodfyn are limited."

"Then you will visit Bodfyn? That's wonderful. Perhaps you'd care to join us for tea tomorrow?"

Lois wasn't sure she wanted to have tea with a couple who visited fatal crash sites for the fun of it. She edged away, leaving Siger to handle the response, and sighed as she heard him respond in the affirmative.

Then something caught her eye.

The coroner had gone back to his car; three AAIB security personnel were at positions on the perimeter; two investigators were studying the point of impact of the propeller and the ground, and two more were kneeling down to sift through scorched debris that had spilled from the cabin of the plane.

Now one of them was standing. He held something in one gloved hand as he carefully brushed away ash with the other.

He consulted a companion, who looked and nodded, and now he came walking back to the van with what he had found.

Lois saw what he was carrying, and for a moment she could not breathe.

It was a necklace—strands of silver, blackened with soot and partially melted from the fire, and a single teardrop sapphire.

Lois recognized it.

It was Laura's.

19

Lois insisted on being at the coroner's office early the following morning, even though the night that led into it had been one of the longest of her life.

That was partly because she had lain on her back worrying about Laura and Reggie. But it was also because Siger, who was supposed to be sleeping on the pullout cot in the front room, had not actually done so, at least so far as Lois could tell.

Instead, almost from the moment Lois had securely closed the bedroom door between them, he had played the violin. And not the cheery, up-tempo pieces he played in the subway for the morning commuters, or the soothing notes he played when the commuters returned from work in the evening. No, it was instead one of the most somber things she had ever heard.

She had finally gotten up and rapped on the door between them. And he had immediately stopped, and then started up again just as soon as she got back to her bed, only now at half volume. Which was to say, just loud enough that she could hear it if she listened for it, which she couldn't help but do, which made it all the more annoying.

Even so, she had made sure that she and Siger were already standing there, in the chilly morning air, when the coroner arrived to open his office.

"Why didn't you wait in your car and stay warm?" asked the coroner as he unlocked the door.

"I wanted to be sure we were here first," said Lois.

Siger, standing next to her, said nothing, but nodded.

The coroner looked at Lois's eyes, saw the shadows below them, and decided not to point out that there was no one else waiting and she might just as well have gotten some sleep. It was clear to him that if she could have slept, she would have.

"My receptionist won't be in for half an hour," said the coroner, as he let them in. "I myself must have some coffee before I do anything else. If you will both have a seat and give me five minutes, and are brave enough, you can share in my best efforts."

"Thank you," said Siger. "I'm sure nothing you do to coffee can make it worse than what I get every morning in the tube station."

"Huh. Personally, when I go to London, I always wait

until I'm out of the tube station to get my coffee, but to each his own. Milk or sugar?"

"Both," said Lois.

"Black," said Siger.

The coroner went through an interior door to the back rooms, and Lois and Siger sat down on green plastic chairs to wait.

The waiting room of the coroner's office was not like that of a doctor's. Or even that of a dentist's. The chairs were not upholstered and there were no gossip magazines. Lois thought it was like the office of an extremely clean auto mechanic—but with no mildly risqué calendar and no car magazines. Just no magazines at all.

There was something to look at, though. On one of the side walls—opposite the one where the coroner had hung his own framed diplomas—was a museum-style display case containing several photos of varying sizes, with type-written index cards pinned next to them.

At the top of the display case was a large label, in magenta block letters, that announced RECENT FINDS.

Siger stood in front of the display and studied it for some minutes, longer than it seemed to warrant, and then he went back and sat down next to Lois.

Siger didn't seem to care about the lack of magazines. He also didn't seem to care about small talk. If he cared about small talk, he would have realized that when two people are not good at it, magazines make it easier for them both not to feel awkward.

Of course, digital devices were just as good for that purpose, or perhaps even better. But Siger wasn't using his.

He was just sitting there with his eyes closed—or at least Lois thought they were—and his fingertips pressed together again.

If he's trying to sleep, she thought, he can join the club.

Now the coroner returned. He brought with him three cups of coffee and his digital tablet. He gave the black coffee to Siger, who finally opened his eyes; he gave the heavily modified one to Lois, who tasted it and decided the coroner had been truthful when he warned them of his coffee-making skills.

The coroner pulled up a plastic chair for himself, sat down facing the two of them, and fired up his digital tablet.

He began to speak in a soft, carefully modulated tone of voice that made it clear to Lois that he had gone into a bedside-manner mode. Or whatever the comparable mode was for coroners. Nice of him to try so hard, she thought.

"I am not at liberty to allow anyone in the general public to view the remains, other than next of kin," said the coroner. "And we still don't know who that might be. I am still in the process of making an identification. However, the accident investigators tell me that you—rather insistently—told them last night that you saw something that would help with that?"

He was asking this of Lois. Siger said nothing. He sampled the coffee and didn't seem to mind the taste of it.

"Yes," said Lois. "Last night. I saw it being carried away from the crash scene."

"Is this a photo of it?"

The coroner showed Lois an image on his tablet.

It was of Laura's necklace—the strands of silver, blackened by fire, and the single teardrop sapphire.

"Yes," said Lois.

"Do you know something about it?"

"I know who wore it. She wore it at her wedding."

"Who did?" said the coroner.

For a moment, Lois could not speak.

"Laura Rankin wore a necklace like that at her wedding," said Siger.

"Laura Rankin the actress?"

"Yes," said Siger. "It's visible in the photos published by the paparazzi, if you need a quick identification. I'm sure there is a jeweler in London who can verify whom he made it for."

"No doubt," said the coroner. "But now that I know where to start, there are more direct means of identification."

"Dental records?" asked Siger.

"Yes."

Lois sniffled, wiped her eyes, and said that she did not know the name of Laura's dentist. Or Reggie's, either. She was sure that Reggie's dentist did not actually go by the names Reggie had for him when return-ing from a visit.

"You needn't worry about that," said the coroner. "I'll take care of it."

Lois took a moment now, and she could hardly bear to look at the coroner as she spoke.

"Do you . . . do you need me to look at the . . . their . . . bodies?"

"No."

"Laura's aunt Mabel and Reggie's brother, Nigel, are the nearest relatives. The only ones that I know of. Will they need to look—"

"No. And I should tell you that to this point we have found the actual remains of only one body. That of a woman."

Lois looked up at the coroner when he said that. So did Siger.

"Do you mean there was only one person in the plane?" asked Siger.

"No, just that so far we have found only one set of re-mains. We have found a man's watch and a belt buckle, but no physiological evidence yet of the man himself. But it's still early in our investigation, and . . . well, skeletal remains can become difficult to recover for a variety of reasons."

"I don't think we should say anything to either Aunt Mabel or Nigel until we know for sure," said Lois. She looked to both the coroner and Siger for confirmation.

Siger nodded.

"Of course," said the coroner. "I suggest you both go back to your hotel and get some rest. I will contact you as soon as we know."

"Thank you," said Lois. "We won't be at the hotel today, though; you'll need to reach us on mobile. We are going to Bodfyn."

"Really?" said the coroner. "There's not much there. I would think you'd be more comfortable here in Amesbury."

"I'm sure you're right," said Lois. "But last night we promised a couple that we would join them for tea."

The coroner frowned.

"You mean a couple you met last night at the crash site?"

"Yes."

"Hmm," said the coroner, with a doctor's noncommittal inflection.

"I try not to renege," said Lois. "And anyway, just waiting in the hotel room to hear word is—well, it's difficult, you know."

The coroner nodded.

"Understood," he said. "I'll contact you by mobile as soon as I know."

Siger paused in the lobby as they walked to the door, and he nodded toward the display cases.

"Is that a hobby?" he asked. "Or official business?"

"Official business," said the coroner. "The Antiquities Act requires—or at least requests, because it's not an easy thing to enforce—that when citizens happen upon historical antiquities in the area, they bring them to the coroner for recording and possible donation to the British Museum or other agencies. As opposed to most people's first instinct, which I think is to rush out and sell them on eBay. I post all the recorded finds in that display."

"Nothing recent, then, I gather," said Siger. "Judging from the age of the photos."

"No, nothing recent," said the coroner. "The last big find of anything new was more than twenty years ago. Now, if there is anything else I can do for you, please don't hesitate . . ."

Siger stopped in the doorway.

"I think many people might imagine that a coroner's practice in such a bucolic area would be a quiet one, but it isn't always, is it?"

"It can be quite busy enough for a part-timer like myself," said the coroner. "I suppose we aren't high on the lists for murder rate, but we have our fatal auto accidents and the occasional drunken drowning. Bird-watchers getting shot on misty mornings by grouse hunters. Food poisonings that have to be investigated to ascertain whether they were indeed just food poisonings, which they always are."

"And the occasional hiker falling into an abandoned quarry on the moor?"

"Ah, yes. You may have read about one of those in the local paper a short time ago. Very sad."

"Haven't seen it," said Siger. "But thank you."

20

You shouldn't have told him where we are going," said Siger quietly as he and Lois got in their car.

"Why?" asked Lois.

"You are too trusting," said Siger.

"The coroner seems quite trustworthy to me," said Lois. She put the car in gear, and they drove out onto the road to Bodfyn.

"To me as well," said Siger. "I simply believe it's not wise to tell anyone your business unless you have a specific reason for wanting the person to know it."

"The specific reason is that I want to know if my best friends have died."

There was a catch in Lois's voice. It registered on Siger, and he just listened as she continued.

"I want the coroner to be able to reach us just as soon as he has definite news. For Aunt Mabel's sake, and for

Nigel's. And for my own. But I'm puzzled what it is that you want."

"I want to know what happened," said Siger.

"Isn't that what I just said?"

"No," said Siger as inoffensively as he could. "Not quite exactly."

With that, he settled back in his seat, pressed his fingertips together again, and closed his eyes.

"Well, end of conversation, then, I guess," said Lois under her breath.

"I heard that," said Siger without changing his posture. "And you're right. But it's only for the moment."

They drove back to their hotel in Amesbury. They got their things, checked out, and got on the road as quickly as possible.

Lois slowed the car as they passed the turnoff to the crash site.

She looked at Siger and asked, rather reluctantly, "Do you want to see it again? In daylight?"

Siger shook his head.

"No need," he said. "I think we should have tea with our new friends."

Lois nodded and they drove on.

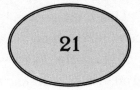

21

They drove under a sky of turquoise blue between the drifting gray and white clouds. But Lois would not allow herself to take pleasure in it. And Siger seemed lost in his own thoughts.

It was not quite noon when they reached the village of Bodfyn.

There was just the one main street. Lois drove it slowly, not wanting to miss their destination.

They passed a pub—the Wayward Pony—a pharmacy, a small auto garage, a grocery. A couple of older men were having a smoke outside the pub; a young woman was leaving the grocery.

As they neared the end of the street, Lois slowed even more, looking to one side.

"Look, they have a theater!"

"Hmm?" Siger roused himself. "Oh. So they do."

"In a town this small?"

Siger nodded. "That is impressive."

"Not my choice of plays, though," said Lois, looking at the banner draped above the doorway. "*Macbeth*. Ugh."

They continued on, reaching the end of the main street. They drove just a bit farther, past the final streetlamp, and took the only turn available, onto a narrow lane.

At the end of it, they found a quaint two-story home with white plaster on the exterior walls, shingles on the slanted roof, and red and purple geraniums in the windows.

Lois stopped the car.

"Yes, I think this is it," said Siger.

"It looks pleasant enough," said Lois.

"Yes," said Siger. "I've had tea in worse places."

"Yes," said Lois, considering it. "I would suppose so."

They walked up the pavers to the entrance, and the door opened just before they could knock.

It was Nancy, from the night before at the crime scene. She wore a bold daytime hat, and a welcoming smile.

"You're right on time!" she said. "I'm so glad to see you. I was worried you might be one of those couples who promise they will come to tea but then don't. What is the word for those kinds of people? I just can't quite remember—"

"Tea teases?" offered Siger.

"Perhaps; the important thing is that you are not them. Thank goodness. Now just come right in; don't be shy.

Roy will be down in just a moment. He'll never say it himself, but he is so hoping you will offer to let him try your tobacco."

Siger raised an eyebrow slightly.

"Oh my, I hope I haven't put my foot in it again. That is tobacco we smelled, isn't it? Well, anyway, mustn't mind anything I say. Just sit right down and I'll get the tea."

Nancy went into the kitchen. Siger and Lois sat down at the little table. It was very pleasant, with white lace place mats and a vase of yellow roses in the center.

Siger checked the contents of his tobacco tin and grimaced, but he said nothing further about it.

Now Nancy returned and poured the tea.

It was Earl Grey. Lois had never liked it; she found the taste of bergamot to be bitter. Their host was so effusively nice, Lois almost thought she might get away with asking for Darjeeling instead.

But no. Shouldn't take advantage. Lois compensated for the bergamot with milk and two teaspoons of sugar.

"So, what brings you both to the little village of Bodfyn?" asked Roy as Nancy passed a small plate of vanilla cream biscuits.

"Your invitation to tea," said Siger. "Or did we misunderstand?"

Nancy laughed.

"No, no, of course not. I think what my husband meant was when we saw you last night."

"We got lost," said Lois quickly, with a subtle glance

at Siger, who seemed to confirm her newly learned caution with an even subtler smile.

"Oh, that's a shame," said Nancy.

"We were headed to Amesbury and took a wrong turn," said Siger.

"No GPS, then?" said Roy.

"We don't believe in that," said Lois helpfully. "Costs extra on a hired car, and next thing you know, it puts you in a lake!"

Roy and Nancy both laughed.

"Oh yes," said Roy, "we have troubles with all this digital technology ourselves."

"You are both Luddites, as well, then?" said Siger.

"Oh no, just pensioners," said Nancy. "Nothing cult-like at all."

"But why Amesbury?" asked Roy quickly. "It's almost as out of the way as Bodfyn, don't you think?"

Siger was about to make up an answer, but Lois got there first.

"Roots!" she said.

Nancy and Roy looked at each other. Siger looked in surprise at Lois.

"Now, do you mean that in a botanical sense," began Roy, rather deliberately, "or do you mean in the sense of ancestry?"

"Botanical!" replied Siger.

"Ancestry!" said Lois at the same time.

Another quick glance between Lois and Siger, and Siger explained.

"That is, she is interested in some heritage sorts of things, and I am a bit of a hobbyist regarding trees. Did you know that some of the oaks in this region are more than five hundred years—"

"Yes," said Roy, interrupting. He seemed much more interested in Lois's response. Turning to her, he asked, "Do you believe you have ancestors in the area?"

"Umm . . . well . . . it's complicated," said Lois.

"Oh?" said Nancy. "Why so?"

"Possibly because there are seventy trillion, three hundred billion, and six hundred and eight possible combinations in the human genome?" said Siger.

"Oh, but they can be mapped, you know," said Nancy. "And how else are you to find out who you really are if you don't know whom you came from?"

"You are what you think, and feel, and do," said Siger. "The genome merely determines the physiological tools you will be born with. And your distant ancestors have even less say in the matter."

Siger sounded annoyed in saying that, and Lois was pretty sure it was because he wasn't happy with the rationale she had given. And now there was an awkward silence, because they had apparently just been rude to their hosts. She hoped that someone would change the subject.

"And what is it that you do, Mr. Siger?" asked Roy.

Lois wasn't sure whether that was changing the subject or not.

"In what context?" said Siger.

"What is your occupation?"

"Oh. That's not quite the same as what I do, of course. My occupation is playing the violin in the Baker Street tube station."

Another silence. Roy and Nancy both looked up from their tea.

"You mean . . . as a sort of hobby?"

"No," said Siger. "Not as a hobby."

Roy and Nancy pondered that for a moment, and then Nancy said, "How does your significant other feel about that?"

Nancy was looking back and forth between Lois and Siger.

Lois laughed, and blushed.

"Oh, he's not my significant other. We're just traveling companions. Anyway, I try not to make occupation the sole criteria. It narrows the possibilities too much."

"Not married?" said Roy.

"No."

"Ever?"

"Oh, stop it, Roy," said Nancy. "That's not polite."

"Oh, yes, I was once, when I was twenty-two," said Lois.

"Ah," said Roy. He seemed very disappointed. Nancy

turned to him and said, "I know, dear, it's just so hard to find someone who qualifies."

Lois tried to fathom the meaning of both Roy's disappointment and Nancy's attempt at consolation, but Nancy quickly distracted her with another question.

"Anyway, I think where we come from is very important. Lois, I presume you have had your Ancestry DNA test done?"

"Umm . . . yes."

It was such a tentative lie—Lois had not had time to prepare for it at all—that she was sure it would be challenged. But it was not.

"And it showed you are descended from someone in this area?" asked Roy, showing surprising interest.

"And is that why you are here?" said Nancy.

"Umm . . . well . . . perhaps."

Roy and Nancy looked at each other and smiled, as though something had just been accomplished, though Lois had no idea what that might be.

Siger suddenly leaned forward.

"So then, what about you two?" said Siger. "What brings you here?"

Roy and Nancy exchanged glances, much as Siger and Lois had a few moments before.

"We came to see a show!" said Nancy.

Roy nodded. "*Macbeth*. It's just a small production, but we are dedicated fans."

"Of the Bard, he means," said Nancy. "The tickets are so much cheaper here than in London."

"I'm sure they are," said Lois.

"And, of course, the accommodations, too. We got this little place through Airbnb," said Nancy. "Can you imagine? It was the first time we ever tried it, and look how well we did! We just showed up, got the key from under the fake rock, and came right in. We did it all online. Didn't even have to talk to the landlady—or an annoying estate agent, or anyone!"

"Well, that's certainly a plus," said Lois. "Estate agents can be so annoying."

"Most definitely," said Roy, nodding.

Siger stirred his tea, studying the milk swirls.

"Landlady?" he said, not looking up.

"Sorry?" said Roy.

"No matter," said Siger, looking up from his tea now. "It is quite a nice place. Two bedrooms, I gather."

"Yes. I believe the advert called them both honeymoon suites," said Nancy.

Roy nudged her and shook his head very slightly. Nancy reacted as if he had reminded her of something, and then she laughed and said, "But of course for Roy and me, that's a bit of a throwback!"

Siger nodded and smiled slightly. He was sitting back in his chair now, seeming to relax a bit for the first time since they had arrived. He took out his pipe. He even opened his tin and offered some to Roy, who accepted, and took out a pipe of his own.

Siger nodded toward the ladies, got their permission— although Lois would have objected if their host hadn't clearly wanted to as well—and lit up.

"Did you see any other offerings in town when you were looking?" he asked.

"Not a one," said Nancy. "I think we were quite lucky. My understanding is this is the only holiday rental in all of Bodfyn!"

"I don't think the town has a hotel, either, does it?"

"Not that we know of."

"Anyone in the other suite?"

"Oh, no, it's been just us from the moment we arrived," said Nancy. Now she looked at Siger and Lois, an idea flashed across her face, and she said, "Oh, do you two need somewhere to overnight? You are certainly welcome to—"

"Oh no," said Lois. "We couldn't—"

"That's a very kind offer," said Siger. "And if it truly is no trouble, we will be grateful to take you up on it."

Lois looked at Siger with alarm, and she kicked his shins under the table.

"I mean, I think we will," said Siger.

Nancy and Roy exchanged puzzled glances.

"I'll start a fresh pot of tea!" said Nancy brightly. She got up and went to the kitchen.

"I'd like to take a look at the unoccupied room, if you

don't mind?" said Siger. "Beggars can't be choosers, of course. I know well. But still—"

"Of course," said Roy. "It's not ours, after all."

As Siger went up the stairs, Nancy came back from the kitchen with the fresh pot of tea.

"You know," she said, "if you're not doing anything tomorrow evening, perhaps you'd care to attend the opening night with us?"

"Well, I suppose that really depends on . . . some other things."

"Oh, do you have other plans?" asked Nancy. "What are they? Perhaps we'll want to do it, too!"

Lois gave a forced laugh. Quite aside from Siger's caution about saying too much, she did not feel like sharing that the plan was to wait and hear whether two of her favorite people in the world had been killed in a plane crash.

"Oh, no, I'm sure that— You know what, I think us attending the play with you might be a lovely idea. I'll just go right upstairs and check with my . . . traveling companion."

Lois went up the short flight of stairs. The door to one of the suites was open, she saw Siger, and she hurried in to join him.

He was standing by the little sofa. He had picked up one of its decorative pillows and was holding it up to his face.

He turned to Lois the moment she entered.

"Shut the door," he said. "I have a question for you."

Lois shut the door.

"The tea downstairs is getting quite complicated," she began, before Siger could ask his own question. "They seem like a very nice couple, but now they want to know if we will—"

Lois stopped. Her mobile was ringing.

She and Siger looked at each other. She picked up.

"Yes, this is Lois."

It was the coroner.

Siger watched Lois's face as she took the call. He heard her short responses, but he didn't need to ask what was being said at the other end of the line. He could read it in her eyes.

All hope went out of them. Lois turned off the phone and steadied herself on the arm of the sofa. Siger caught her there and sat her down.

She made no noise as she cried. The tears ran silently.

She looked at Siger, who was kneeling beside her, the damn silly pillow in his hand.

"He confirmed it," said Lois. "From Laura's dental records."

Siger just stared as she said that. Then he said, "My question for you . . ."

"What?" Lois practically screamed at him. What question could possibly matter?

"Smell this," said Siger. He held the pillow in front of her.

"What are you . . . I don't want . . ."

"Please. Just smell it."

Lois sniffed, or tried to. She sniffled. Siger gave her a tissue and she blew her nose. Then she sniffed the pillow again.

"Do you recognize it?"

She stared back at Siger.

"What? The . . . the perfume?"

Siger nodded.

"Is it familiar?"

"I . . . think so. But I'm not sure where—"

"In the underground," said Siger, "early in the morning, before all the scents get jumbled—I can smell the perfume on the women who pass by, and especially on those who stop for a moment to make a contribution. I've learned to recognize those scents. Not by name, of course—I'd have to go to a perfume counter for that—but by the style and kind of women who wear them. Some scents are more expensive than others. Some are worn by younger women, some by older, some by women comfortable with their age, and some by women who are less so. Women who are having affairs, or hoping to, and women who are not. Some by short women, some by tall women, some by famous red-haired independent-minded beauties—they all tend to self-select for particular scents. I don't know how, but they do."

Lois was beginning to understand his point, but she still stared back with disbelief.

"Who do you know who wears this scent?" asked Siger.

"It's a very expensive scent. And not at all common. Do you know it?"

Lois blinked, sniffled again and wiped her nose, then said, "Laura has it. She wore it at the wedding. I know, because I asked her about it."

Siger nodded and stood.

"Yes," he said. "Laura Rankin wore it at her wedding. And someone very recently wore it here."

Lois blinked, trying to comprehend the implications of that.

But now there was a knock on the bedroom door, and Roy called in to them.

"So, what do you think? Is it satisfactory?"

Lois cleared her throat and called out that it was quite nice.

Siger opened the door.

"It was a lovely tea," said Lois when they got back downstairs. She picked up her coat. "Thank you very much."

"Oh, you are most welcome. Must you leave so soon?"

"There are some roots I want to look at," said Siger. "The black oak that I was telling you about."

"I hope you will be back in time to join us at the theater."

"We will do our very best," said Siger.

"It would be a shame to miss it. Everyone in town is going. Absolutely everyone will be there, and—oh my—dear, are you all right? Did I say something wrong?"

"No, no," said Lois. "I'm fine, really. We will certainly join you at the theater if we can. I do so love that play."

They made their way to the door.

"Well. We're very glad to have run into you," Roy said, "and we'll be thrilled if you decide to take the other room upstairs."

"Yes. It's so important to have a good backup ready, just in case," said Nancy.

"The room, we mean, of course," said Roy, "in case you don't find another."

"Yes," said Nancy. "That's exactly what I meant."

Siger and Lois went to the car, Siger opened the door on the driver's side, and he was about to get in himself.

"What are you doing?" asked Lois.

"You are in no condition to drive," he said.

"You said you haven't driven in twenty years!"

"I haven't."

"Then go back to your own side. I'm still driving," said Lois. With an effort, she stopped sniffling.

"As you wish," said Siger.

"Where are we going?"

"Back to the coroner," said Siger.

Siger got in the passenger side, and Lois sat down behind the wheel. She sniffled once more, blew her nose, took a breath, and then floored the accelerator, peeling out onto the road.

They were about to pass by the theater on their way out of town.

"Slow down," said Siger.

"I'm fine, and I'm driving," said Lois.

"I mean that I want to look at something," said Siger.

"What?"

"Just a bit slower, please. No need to stop."

She slowed. Siger rolled his window down and stared out at the theater entrance as they passed by.

"What?" said Lois again.

Siger shook his head dismissively.

"Nothing important," he said. "Their playbill shows a casting change, is all. Let's go talk to the coroner. And you may drive as fast as you like."

22

Lois took the winding curves at a speed that gave Siger white knuckles from gripping the armrest, but even so, it was late afternoon when they reached Amesbury.

If there was anything more to know, Lois wanted to know it now, and not struggle through the night with doubts. She was relieved to see that there were still other vehicles in the small car park as they pulled up.

They entered the coroner's reception area. Again it was empty, and no receptionist, but the door to the inner office was open, and Lois knocked on it.

The coroner was at his desk. He looked up, saw who it was, and waved them both in.

"I am sorry," he said. "I know this is not the news you were hoping for. We still have not found physiological evidence of the passenger in the plane. But we have identified the pilot."

On his desk he had a large white envelope with the official markings of Her Majesty's Judiciary Branch; from it he pushed several high-gloss photographs of someone's teeth and jawbones.

Lois began to feel sick at the pit of her stomach. She looked away.

Now he took a yellow clasp envelope out of a drawer, opened it, and slid four narrow sheets of celluloid out onto his desk. They were dark around the edges, shiny gray a bit farther in, and white where the images of the teeth appeared. He tapped them lightly—almost patting them— as if it might make Lois feel better.

"These are very old," said Siger almost immediately, leaning in for a better look.

"Yes," said the coroner.

"Why?" asked Siger. "Has it been decades since Ms. Rankin has been to the dentist?"

"No, of course not," said the coroner, and now he looked at Lois. "But I knew you wanted an answer as soon as possible, and all of the students who attended the boarding school were treated by the only dentist who was in town at that time. His practice still exists here, and we were fortunate to find that all of the students' dental records—including those of Ms. Rankin— are still in the archived files. So rather than require you to wait until her dentist in London can be found, I thought you would prefer to see what we have immediately."

Lois hesitated.

"Does that even work?" she began. "I mean, what about baby teeth, and crowns, and—"

"All of an adult's permanent teeth are in well before the age of fourteen, which is the age Ms. Rankin was when she had her last exam by the local dentist," said the coroner. "And although fillings and other dental work can continue, of course, throughout one's life, there were more than enough positive matches here to make an identification—biting surfaces, the shape and angle of the roots, all a perfect match."

Lois was silent, and tensely trying to hold it together.

Siger stopped staring at the old X-ray sheet and looked up.

"I suppose that back in the day," he said, "the local dentist may have had as many clients at the school as in the town itself."

"Quite so," said the coroner. "He found it necessary to keep offices in both locations. He treated both faculty and students at the school, and they accounted for more than half his practice."

The coroner struggled desperately for something more to say.

"The records show that Ms. Rankin always had truly excellent teeth, by the way, if that's . . . any . . . consolation. I mean, knowing that she never had a bad time at the dentist is something. . . ."

"What?" said Lois.

"I'm sorry; that was just a ridiculous thing for me to say," said the coroner.

"No, no," said Lois, "I mean, I wasn't paying attention, really. Just . . . thinking. What to do next. What to . . . say to her aunt. What to—"

Lois turned suddenly to Siger.

"What about the perfume thing?" she began. "Do we need to ask—"

Siger shook his head emphatically.

"What perfume thing?" asked the coroner.

"Oh," said Lois, "we just . . . uh—"

"We will report back to Ms. Rankin's aunt," said Siger quickly, "and then she will be in touch. Thank you once again for your time."

Siger stood, clearly now in a hurry to leave, and Lois took the hint. The coroner got up from his desk as they proceeded from his office into the lobby.

"If there is anything else I can do . . ."

"Thank you so very much," said Lois.

Lois and Siger went out to the car. Lois got behind the wheel again—wordlessly—and she to began to take the turn toward the main road.

"Wait!" said Siger suddenly. "Stop the car."

"Aren't we going back to Aunt Mabel's?"

"Not yet."

Lois pulled to the curb.

"Do you have a hard copy of the wedding photo? The one I saw on your computer at Baker Street?

"I . . . well, yes," said Lois.

"Get it out, please," said Siger.

Lois went to the boot of the car, opened the one bag she had packed, and brought out the desk photo of the wedding couple.

When she got back to the front seat with it, she saw that Siger had taken a jeweler's magnifying glass out of his coat pocket.

Under other circumstances, she might have regarded that as pretentious. Right now, she was too distressed to think of that.

"Thank God for Ms. Rankin's toothy smile," said Siger as he took the photo.

He held the magnifier up close against the photo for a long moment, adjusting it very slightly.

Then he sighed and put both items down.

"Inconclusive," he said. "Now we'll have to go to the dentist's."

"Why?" asked Lois. "We just saw the X-rays, didn't we?"

"It will only take a moment," said Siger.

They drove toward the center of town and found the dental office at the end of a row of converted eighteenth-century town houses.

"It's closed," said Lois as they drove up.

"No matter," said Siger.

He got out of the car and went first to the front door and then, very quickly, around to the side. There he spent a few seconds more, bending over to look closely at the door lock.

Then he came back.

He was almost smiling. Lois could see that he was quite energized about something.

"What?"

"It's good news," said Siger. "Not conclusive, and you mustn't get your hopes up."

"What?" repeated Lois.

"Their lock has been picked, and recently," said Siger. "They have been burglarized—and my guess is they don't even know it."

Lois considered that.

"What do we do now? Go to the police?"

"What? Oh, my dear woman, no. Not until we have finished our chores. We have talked to the doctor. We have been to the dentist's. Now we must go to the school."

23

They stayed on the main road, bypassing Bodfyn, and made their way as quickly as possible to the school.

Even so, it was near dusk when they arrived.

As Lois pulled to a stop in the empty car park, her strongly ingrained sense of the proprieties reasserted itself.

"Don't forget, we promised that couple we would meet them at the theater," she said as Siger jumped out of the car.

Siger looked back with a quizzical expression, then nodded dismissively and began walking quickly around the south end of the school.

"Wait," called Lois. "Wait for me."

He slowed his pace only slightly, and she ran to catch up.

"Why not try the front entrance first?" she said. "Are you afraid it will be more heavily secured?"

"No," said Siger. "Or, rather, yes, it will be, but I'm

hardly afraid of that; an estate agent's lock is not much of a deterrent. But we are in a hurry. The medical annex of a boarding school—and so, of course, the medical and dental records cabinets, as well—is typically located between the main entrance, where prospective students are received and then sent for proper examination, and the gymnasium, where injuries are most likely to occur, and it's typically at the end of one of the buildings, for easier access from the dormitories, as well, which means that—ah, yes, here we are."

They had tromped around to the south end of the main building. To their left was the gymnasium—they knew this because it had a sign indicating that here was the entrance to the girls' locker room, the boys' being, presumably, at the other side of the building.

To their right was a side door to the main building; it was not labeled, but Siger seemed sure of the location as he manipulated a thin metal tool in the lock.

"A bit of rust," said Siger, by way of an apology for the delay, and then the lock fell open.

He grabbed the door handle and pulled.

Nothing happened.

Lois stepped up and gave the low outer corner of the door a good swift kick.

Siger pulled again, and now the door opened with a high-pitched moan.

"A bit of rust there, too," said Lois.

Siger was about to step inside.

"Wait," said Lois. "Are you sure there is no one else around?"

"Who would be here?"

"It's for sale. Prospective buyers?"

"Not likely at this hour. Ours is the only vehicle here, and we're not within walking distance of anything."

"I know, but—"

"But what?"

"I thought I heard something."

Siger turned away from the doorway and faced Lois.

"Heard what?"

"I'm not sure. It sounded rather like . . . some sort of pounding."

"I didn't hear anything," said Siger, glancing back at the entrance. "But, of course, I've spent the past five years in a subway tunnel."

"You were on the other side of the door," said Lois. "I don't think it came from that building."

"From where, then?"

Lois pointed at the gymnasium building.

"That one."

"Are you sure?"

"No."

"Do you hear it now?"

"I don't know," said Lois. She raised her hand. "Be quiet a minute, and let's see."

They both said nothing and listened as hard as they could for several seconds.

"Well?" said Siger.

Lois shook her head.

"I don't hear anything now. Do you?"

"No," said Siger. "Are you sure you actually heard anything at all?"

"How should I know?" said Lois. "I'm not sure of anything. My best friends are dead. I haven't slept for an hour straight in the past two days. I'm cold and tired and hungry and everything wrong is my fault. How the bloody hell do I know if I'm hearing things or not?"

"Now, Lois," began Siger, and then he stopped, because he really wasn't used to this sort of thing. "There, there," he said, and he realized he should have been patting her back or something as he said it, but she was several feet away, and it seemed like a difficult thing to do, somehow, under the circumstances.

"Now, Lois," he said, trying again, "you . . . we . . . you mustn't give up hope."

"Why the bloody hell not?"

"Because there is always hope. Or, to put a finer point on it, there almost always is, and since we can never be completely certain when there is and when there isn't, it is always necessary to think and feel and behave as though there is. If you follow me."

Lois had started sniffling again. Siger began to realize that this was usually a good sign—the sniffling seemed to follow the worst of the emotional crisis more often than to precede it.

"Oh, all right," said Lois. "Let's just get on with it, then. Here. It looks like we'll need my torch."

Lois produced a small LED flashlight from her purse. Siger, already standing in the dark entryway, accepted it and went in first.

They were in a long corridor; it was too dark to know any more than that. Siger used the flashlight to find a wall switch, and he flipped it, but no light came on.

"I don't see how they can expect to sell the place with the electricity off," said Lois.

"Perhaps it's the bulbs, or perhaps off at the main switch," said Siger. "But I don't think we will have to go far."

Siger shone the light first on the floor ahead of them to see where they would be putting their feet, and then on the walls, searching for a doorway and a nameplate.

Within a few feet of the entrance, they found a narrow door that opened on just a janitor's closet—and the view and scent of an old and moldy mop.

They moved on for several more feet to another closed door, a full-size one this time, on the opposite side of the corridor. Siger brushed dust away from a nameplate near the door.

"We've found it," he said.

He turned the door handle easily enough, and then had to give the door a push. It opened with a shudder.

They surveyed the room with the flashlight.

It was the patient lobby for the infirmary.

The chill air and the limited scope of the flashlight made it feel eerie, but beneath the accumulated dust, Lois could see orange and blue plastic chairs, a linoleum tile in a pattern that at one time would have been regarded as friendly and calming, and a bulletin board that still had helpful cartoon-character tips about personal hygiene tacked to it.

There were end tables next to several chairs, and unlike the waiting room at the coroner's office, this waiting room had reading material.

A *Boys' Life* magazine. A very tame teen glamour mag. Someone's homework with a cheery "Well Done!" marked in violet felt pen. A yearbook.

Lois was curious, for no particular reason that she was aware of, and she would have looked closer at some of this, but now Siger aimed the light on a short hallway that extended from the waiting room to the interior offices.

The first two, as expected, turned out to be medical exam offices, and then a medical storage closet, and then, finally, the dental office.

Siger went first. The door opened easily, he aimed the flashlight at the center of the room—and then he screamed.

Not a loud scream, not sustained, and not high-pitched by any means, more like just a guttural gasp, if you had asked his opinion, but it was a scream nonetheless.

He dropped the flashlight, and the entire corridor went

dark. Lois bumped into Siger as she moved forward to help.

What?" she said. "What's wrong?"

"I'm sorry," said Siger. "I apologize, and if we had time for me to be embarrassed, I would be. I'll just admit it: I can abide the sight of almost anything in medicine, but not the sight or sound of the dentist's drill."

"Oh," said Lois. "Goodness. It only hurts a little. I took you to be someone a little more stoic than that."

"Oh, it's not the physical pain. It's the bad memories."

"You should have had them knock you out, then. That's what I do, almost as soon as I get in the chair."

"No, no, you don't understand. I wasn't in the chair. I was the one with the drill. I tried dental school for a bit after I was booted from my medical internship. I went overseas to the States. They had a program where they train you on low-income dental patients, and—"

"Oww, oww, oww," said Lois.

"Yes," said Siger. "I heard that a lot. As I said, bad memories. I couldn't take it, had to drop out."

"Uh-huh," said Lois. "Well, can you abide going in now—assuming you didn't break our only light?"

Siger nodded, then cleared his throat and said yes, remembering that she could not see him in the dark.

Lois, on her hands and knees, finally found the little flashlight. She shook it, pushed it, twisted it—and amazingly, it came back on.

This time, Lois went into the room first.

"Look on the back wall and corners," said Siger. "It's the file cabinet that we want."

Lois scanned the back wall with the light until she found it—a double file cabinet in the corner to their right.

"Do you really think they have the X-rays that far back?" asked Lois.

Siger went to the file cabinets eagerly.

"They might well have," he said. "The film is very thin."

He opened the first drawer, and Lois aimed the light into it.

Empty. Not a film, not an envelope, not a hanging folder.

"Nothing," said Lois.

Siger tried the next drawer, with the same result. Then the next. And then the next.

"Blast," said Siger. "I had hoped to find either Ms. Rankin's original X-ray or an indication that it had been deliberately removed. But this tells us nothing."

Lois lowered the flashlight, almost dropping it.

"I told you there was no hope," she said. She turned away and went back into the corridor, toward the lobby, not even bothering to raise the flashlight, and bumping into walls as she went.

"Please," said Siger, following. "At least raise it up a bit."

She did so. They'd reached the waiting room now, and she had to raise the flashlight to find the door.

As she did, the light glanced on something else.

"What was that?" said Siger.

"What?"

"In the corner."

"Oh," said Lois. "I saw that earlier. They tried to make it very comfortable here for the students, I think. Gave them something to look at while they waited. Magazines and such."

"But that hardbound one on top, with photos of the school—"

"A yearbook, of course," said Lois.

"A yearbook," repeated Siger. "Of course. That could show us. Where would the school have kept its older yearbooks, do you suppose?"

"The library?" said Lois. "But show us what?"

"The fourteen-year-old Laura Rankin," said Siger. "Would you expect that the library would be located toward the center of the building, to be close to all the classrooms, and to be a centerpiece for visitors?"

"I would," said Lois.

They started out in that direction through the main corridor, moving as quickly as they could with their limited light, and taking it more or less on faith that the estate agents had kept the corridor clear of debris.

Some ten minutes later, they reached the main lobby, and adjacent to that was the library. It had wide double doors, heavy and ornate, like the lobby itself, and they were open.

They found the yearbooks—three shelves of them—on the wall behind the reference desk.

"We want one from the same year as the dental records," said Siger. "Back twenty years, to the fourteen-year-old Laura Rankin."

Siger quickly sorted through and pulled that volume from the shelf. He placed it open on a table, and Lois held the flashlight over it and they flipped through the pages.

They turned to the galleries of student photos for each grade level, and went through them in alphabetical order until they found Laura Rankin's head shot.

There she was—no more than fourteen years old, and all red hair, freckles, and a wide smile of beautifully straight teeth.

"Hmm," said Siger.

"What?"

"The same teeth as in her wedding photo."

"Is that good or bad?"

Siger hesitated.

"It's . . . well . . . it means that the naturally perfect roots of the teeth I saw in the X-rays from the dental work are consistent with the general shape of the perfect teeth in this shot and in the wedding photo."

"Oh," said Lois, and she realized from his tone of voice, as much as the words, that it was not good. "You are saying . . . that it is indeed Laura."

Siger did not answer immediately.

"These head-shot galleries," he asked after a moment, "at what point during the year do you suppose they were taken?"

"At the very end, usually," said Lois. "Just before graduating from that particular grade level."

Siger nodded.

"Yes," he said. "And that was many months later, because the date on the X-rays was September of the year. We need an earlier comparison."

He began to flip through more pages, passing through the section of head shots and into the activities sections.

He reached a two-page spread decorated with cheery white and gold snowflakes and headlined WINTER HOLIDAY DANCE.

He stopped. Lois followed his hand as it moved across to the second page of the spread and stopped on one particular photo.

"That's her!" said Lois. "That girl caught slow-dancing with that chubby boy!"

"Yes," said Siger. "And look closely!"

Lois did so.

"You know," said Lois, "he does look vaguely familiar somehow, but I just can't quite—"

"No, not him!" said Siger. "Laura! Look at her mouth!"

Lois did. It was that same wide smile—except just a bit wider perhaps, due to astonishment and embarrassment, and except for something shiny and—

"Braces!" cried Lois.

"Yes," said Siger. "The perfectly aligned teeth that Laura Rankin happily displays in her wedding photo were not at all perfect twenty years ago. I don't know whose perfect teeth we see in the X-ray and in the remains from the plane, but they are not hers."

24

Lois and Siger exited the building in the same way they had come in—but in much better spirits, especially for Lois.

Siger noticed. He smiled slightly but made no comment. Lois had been so focused on Laura—standing in, in effect, for Laura's aunt—that they had not had time to talk about Reggie.

Hope was one thing, but Siger was still a realist—and his instinct told him something remained dreadfully wrong.

He had learned over the years, sometimes at great cost, not to ignore his instinct. Perhaps that inner voice was the sum of so many subtle and subconscious bits of experience and knowledge that it simply wasn't possible to pick one out by itself and identify it as the reason for concern. Or perhaps it was some sort of inherited genetic instinct, or something more.

But the source of it wasn't important. Siger paused for a long moment after they emerged, standing between the main building, from which they had just come, and the gymnasium building a few feet away.

"Your hearing is excellent, is it not?" he said to Lois.

"Yes."

"Did you hear anything just now, after we shut the door?"

Lois paused. She listened carefully. She heard nothing.

"No," she said. "I thought you said you are partially deaf?"

"I am," he said.

"Oh," said Lois, looking at her watch. "It is nearly seven. We promised Roy and Nancy we would meet them for the play. I suppose we could cancel."

"No," said Siger. "No, I think we should go. Mustn't be rude."

25

The road back to town was not long, but it was a country road at night, with no streetlamps at all. Lois tried the high beams, which weren't adjusted well, then the low beams, which didn't illuminate far enough ahead, and then she went back to the high beams again.

Siger had the yearbook in his lap as she drove; he flipped through the pages, trying to look closely at them with Lois's flashlight.

"What about Reggie?" asked Lois quite suddenly.

"I don't know," said Siger. "But I'm convinced that someone switched Laura's X-rays at the dental office. Or at the coroner's, if the picked lock at the dental office was faked to throw us off. Either way, someone wants it to seem that they both died in that plane crash."

"Then they are both still alive?" said Lois.

Siger did not respond immediately, then said, "There is always hope."

They drove silently for several moments. A wind had come up, driving clouds in front of the moon, making the road and surroundings darker yet. It was nearly pitch-black.

"We haven't seen a single other car," said Lois.

Siger looked up from the yearbook.

"Interesting," he said. "Nothing in either direction?"

"No," said Lois. "Nothing."

"Not so much as a pair of taillights ahead of us at any point?"

"No," said Lois. "I suppose I could drive real fast and see if we can find some."

"No," said Siger.

But now he closed the yearbook and began to pay attention to the drive.

No vehicles ahead. None behind. None approaching from the opposite direction.

Not all that unusual, really, for such a country road, late at night.

But it really wasn't all *that* late.

Siger tried to peer into the dark terrain on the side of the road where he had seen some distant farmhouses on the drive out. For more than a mile, he saw nothing but black night. Then, finally, he saw one single whitish stationary light—a porch light, probably—at the base of a distant rise. It was just the one light, though—no interior light that you would expect to see in an occupied farmhouse so early in the evening.

"I suppose I've been living in the city too long," said Siger. "These country roads seem dark to me now."

"Did you ever live in the country?" asked Lois.

"Certainly," said Siger. "I had a little farm once."

"Of course. I don't know why I wondered."

"But even after my most exhausting days, I would stay up for a while in the evening. Not immediately turn out the lights. It feels as though it's midnight, but it's barely after seven."

Now, far off on the opposite side of the road, something caught his eye. A yellow-orange flicker. Just one, quite distant, all by itself.

A flame?

But it was in lateral motion. And now it was gone. Whether extinguished, or gone behind some obstruction, or whether it had just been some figment of Siger's blinking vision, he could not now tell.

They came over the final rise above Bodfyn. The town was immediately identifiable by its two streetlamps, one at each end. As they drew closer, Siger saw the same oddity that he had seen in the countryside. Everyone seemed to have called it a night.

Lois noticed it, too.

"Has everyone gone to bed or something? Even the Fish and Chips looks closed."

"I don't know," said Siger. "Let's stop at the pub and ask."

"I think even they are closing," said Lois as they pulled up.

Indeed, the bartender was outside, just now shutting the front door.

"Are we too late for a pint?" asked Siger, jumping out of the car.

"You're late, period. Everyone is already at the theater."

"We're heading there, too," said Siger, "but I've never seen an entire town shut down for that purpose."

"It's bloody nonsense if you ask me," said the bartender with undisguised irritation. "They'll never reopen that school. It's too far away from everything, and costs have gone up too much. And they can't raise enough money to buy it by putting on a play, either. It's like having a bake sale to buy the crown jewels. It'll sell to some toff for his country estate, and that will be that."

"For what it's worth, I agree with you," said Siger. "Why do you think they're trying it, then?"

"How should I know? What I do know is, the pub is the true heart of a village; everyone knows that. Yet here it is Saturday, we're the only pub in town, and we're closing for this?"

"It's your pub," said Lois. "Why don't you just stay open?"

The bartender shook his head.

"Wouldn't do any good. Everyone in town is at the play. Or will be, as soon as you two get there. Not that I blame you for dallying. *Macbeth*? Could they have picked anything more of a downer? Damn long play, too, I hear. I wouldn't mind so much, though, if they still had their guest star."

"Guest star?"

"Laura Rankin. Beautiful woman. Came in the other night with her husband—some legal wanker."

"Reggie Heath was a QC," said Lois defiantly. "And he was only a wanker when the duties of his profession required him to be. And besides that, he loved Laura."

"Just married they said, if you can believe that," said the bartender. He shook his head in longing and disapproval of the choice the lady had made. And then, uncharacteristically observant for some reason, he added, "Did you say 'was'?"

"No," said Lois. She certainly had not intended to use the past tense.

"I knew her, you know. Back in my school days," continued the bartender. "We were both in the eleventh form, when she was still Laura Penobscott. Much better looking than her surname suggests, even then. I mean, once the braces were off. I took her out in the meadow once and showed her how much she meant to me by carving her initials in one of the rocks. I was going to carve mine in, too, but we got interrupted, and I didn't want to put my signature on something I hadn't completed, if you know what I mean."

Lois rolled her eyes.

"I've never forgiven that teacher, spoiling my action like that. He's still hanging around, you know, comes into the pub now and then, fluffing his white hair out, acting like he's better than the rest of us. But I'll tell you, back in the day, if he hadn't come along when he did—well, I used to give lessons, too, if you know what I mean."

Siger suspected that Lois might be annoyed by that remark, and he wouldn't blame her, but he wasn't quick enough to caution her to stay on point.

"Please stop ending your statements with that phrase," said Lois. "Everyone knows what you think you mean."

The bartender didn't pick up on her tone of voice.

"Chemistry is chemistry, as far as I'm concerned, and I say it never goes away. If she had only stayed around to do the play, there's no telling what might have—"

"Nonsense," said Lois. "I don't believe you ever had a shot at Laura Rankin or Laura Penobscott, either one. You are entitled to your fantasies, of course, but you needn't inflict them on us."

Lois glared; the bartender finally knew to shut his mouth, and he began to turn away.

"Wait," said Siger. "What did you mean about staying to do the play?"

"The play," said the bartender. "That Macbeth thing, I told you, what they're shutting the town down for."

"Yes, yes, but—you said she was to be in it, but now isn't?"

"Right, like I said."

"Do you know what happened? Why Ms. Rankin is no longer in the play?"

The bartender shrugged.

"Beats me. It's just what I heard. Excuse me, I have to go lock up in back."

"One moment," said Siger. "I notice you have a viewing deck in the back. That is a telescope I see near the railing, isn't it?"

"Of course."

"We had very much hoped to have a look. Could we do so perhaps, before you close up?"

"Sorry, no. I'm closing up, as I said."

"Very well, if you must. But could you at least tell us, though, what the view is?"

"Nothing, if you ask me," said the bartender. "Just a couple of hills and a bit of the valley between, and you can't see anything at all in the dark."

"Understood," said Siger. "We'll just try another time."

The bartender nodded, glad to be rid of them, and went back inside.

"Why do we want to see the view?" asked Lois as they went back to their car.

"I'm still working on that," said Siger. "What seems

clear to me is that someone has gone to some trouble to make sure that no one at all sees it tonight."

They drove on to the theater.

The modest car park next to the onetime church was full and overflowing, with a number of sedans and small farm trucks parked on the shoulder of the main road. Lois backed the car up, turned it around, and parked along the shoulder, as well.

They hurried up to the entrance.

Standing at the entrance, peering around like sentries, were Roy and Nancy. They both smiled broadly when they saw Lois and Siger.

"Glad you could make it!" said Roy, coming down the steps to greet them.

"We were about to send out a search party!" said Nancy.

"We were a bit worried we'd be late ourselves," said Lois.

"What kept you?" said Roy.

"Nothing of importance," said Siger as he and Roy shook hands. And then, when he released Roy's hand, Siger said, "I think you should fire your manicurist."

"Excuse me?"

"Personally, I would find it inconvenient, perhaps even painful, to have my nails cut back that short."

"Ah, yes," said Roy, looking at his own fingertips as though he had just discovered the issue. "I wish now that I hadn't tipped her."

"Hmm," said Siger.

"Well, come on in, then!" said Nancy. "We saved seats for you, front row!"

"Thank you so much," said Lois. "Front row for *Macbeth*. I do hope the witches spit carefully!"

Lois gave Siger a look to indicate her true feelings, but she dutifully started forward.

Siger stepped behind to let her go first.

"Owww!" said Lois.

"Oh, I'm so sorry," said Siger.

"You stepped on my foot!"

"Oh dear," said Nancy.

"Very clumsy of me, no doubt," said Siger.

"Oh my," said Nancy. "Do you need to come in and get a bandage?"

"No, no, I'm fine. But he broke my heel."

"So sorry," said Siger again. "We'd better just go back to the car and get your other pair."

"What other—"

Lois caught Siger's glance, and she stopped.

"Oh. Yes. The pair I stowed in the boot. Well, lucky I did that."

"The play is about to start," warned Roy.

"We'll just be a moment," said Siger. "You can go on in yourselves; just leave the door unlocked, and we'll be right in."

Siger put his hand under Lois's arm as if for support and hurried her back across the pavers to the car.

"What?" said Lois along the way. "What's going on?"

Siger waited until they had almost reached the car and were completely out of earshot. He glanced back at the entrance, where Roy was still waiting, holding the door. Siger waved, held up two fingers to indicate how long they would be, and then opened the boot, as if to find Lois's shoes.

At the entrance, Roy nodded and finally went inside.

"What?" said Lois again.

"When we met them for tea," said Siger, "I noticed some fine yellowish dirt deep under Roy's fingernails. Like the dirt in the local fields. There was just a bit of it, a fine layer well under the fingernails, that he hadn't been able to clean out. It's why I asked him about being from the British Museum."

"Oh," said Lois. "It wasn't just the tie?"

"No. And as you recall, he said he is retired, not on a dig, and hasn't been on one in ages."

"He lied," said Lois.

"Yes. And not only did he lie initially but he went to the trouble since then of trying to cover up by cutting his own fingernails so closely that they almost bled."

"Are you sure? Oh, don't tell me. I suppose you were a manicurist at one time?"

"No. I dated one."

Lois just stared at Siger for a brief moment.

"What?" said Siger.

"Nothing, nothing. I was just . . . trying to imagine.

But why? Assuming you are right, why would he cut his fingernails so short?"

"Exactly." Siger nodded. "That's the question. Would you get the yearbook from the front seat, please? And come around the other side; if they come back to the door, we want them to see only that we are looking in the boot with your torch. You must look as though you are still hunting for your spare shoes."

"I am hunting for my spare shoes," said Lois. "Or I will be shortly. It's no fun walking on one heel."

Lois got the yearbook and flashlight. Siger opened the boot, they set the yearbook down inside it, and as Lois shone the light, Siger flipped through to the two-page spread showing Laura's Winter Holiday Dance photo.

The spread was not all just about Laura, of course. Lois and Siger saw the photo of the banner that proclaimed the occasion for the dance, the photo of the streamers and the glitter ball, the photos of the two teacher chaperones, and of all the other students present at the ball, in a whole slew of awkward poses.

And beneath each photo was a caption—in a typeface so small that it was barely noticeable, and not readable at all from just a quick glance.

"You said you recognized someone," said Siger.

"No, I said one looked familiar."

"Which one?"

"This one. The chubby boy with the acne and the embarrassed look dancing with Laura."

"Hmm. I suspect you're right; I suspect you do know him. However, I saw someone else on this page that looks familiar as well, and I am quite certain about the one that I recognize. But of course it's not a fair contest. I think you are trying to match a photo with someone whom you have only seen for the first time some twenty years later. Whereas I have the advantage of seeing my subject in two photos taken within a relatively short time of each other."

"Who?"

"This one," said Siger. "The adult chaperone standing here by the exit. I saw a photo of him somewhere else—on the wall in the coroner's office. It showed him standing in front of the artifact discovery that was reported to the coroner twenty years ago."

"This was the man who discovered those stones?"

"Yes."

"All right," said Lois. "One of Laura's teachers at the boarding school made an archaeological discovery nearby. Is that important?"

"I would not have thought so," said Siger, "if someone had not lied to us about being near that site, and if someone had not gone to the trouble of switching dental records to make it appear as though Laura died in the plane crash."

Siger stared at the yearbook photos a moment longer, and said, "So we have an archaeological discovery not very far from the school, in a field that is referred to in one of the other student photos as 'Romeo's Meadow.' No doubt our bartender friend is familiar with the location. Now look at this boy in the 'Winter Holiday' photo, standing along the wall, watching Laura dance."

"Why—that's him, isn't it? Our bartender."

"Yes. Tell me what emotion you see on his face; I'll take your word for it."

"Oh my," said Lois. "Someone wants Laura who can't have her."

"My interpretation, as well," said Siger. "But he's not the only one. Who else? I mean just from these photos?"

"Well, I would say the embarrassed boy rather likes her, too," said Lois, "judging from the way he's trying to stretch his pants pocket out to disguise his . . . obvious indicator."

"I think there's one more interested party," said Siger. "Look closely at these other two shots—this one, where you see the male chaperone watching Laura slow-dance, and this one, where he is glaring at the other boy who is watching her slow-dance."

"Oh my," said Lois. "That's a look."

"Yes," said Siger. "Of some kind."

"I don't know quite how to describe it, but it certainly creeps the bloody hell out of me."

"Agreed. Now, the photo that looks familiar to you— the boy dancing with Laura— Here, I'll hold the light; you check the caption."

Lois looked at the caption.

"It says his name is 'Potty Bobby.' Oh, that's just mean.

Didn't they have any supervision on this yearbook? Wait, there's more. His real name is—"

Lois gasped.

"My God," she said. "I can't believe it. Him? Really? He's done nothing but give Reggie and Laura grief, and I think he's just the biggest—"

Suddenly, Siger slammed the boot closed and called out toward the theater entrance.

"Still looking! Any minute now!"

Lois turned and saw what Siger had seen: Roy had come back outside and was staring across at them, and now Nancy joined him, pointing at Lois and Siger. Nancy and Roy began a rather animated conversation between themselves.

"Why are they so bloody determined for us to join them?" said Lois under her breath as she looked back at them.

"I have a theory," said Siger. "I hope I'm wrong, but if I'm right, we have very little time. I will have to go into the theater."

"But—"

"I can delay it, I think. I used to be an actor, after all, but—"

"Delay what?"

"Well, I . . . it's only a theory, mind you, but when you have eliminated the impossible, whatever remains, however unlikely—"

Lois interrupted him.

"And what do you mean, 'used to be an actor'? Isn't there any occupation that you haven't previously—"

"Very few," said Siger. "But we haven't much time. You must hurry. Drive as fast as you can—I know you can do that. As soon as you get a connection, call Potty Bobby, tell him who needs him, and that he must come immediately with all the help he can muster. Here are the coordinates to give him. You could mention Romeo's Meadow as a reference point, but perhaps he won't know exactly where it is. I'm guessing that, unlike our bartender, he didn't get to make much use of it back in the day."

"Now that we know who he is, I very much doubt that he'll take my call," said Lois. "He's never much liked Baker Street Chambers, you know."

"No, the thing he didn't like was competition for Laura. He will come, if you explain. Drag him out of his Wapping castle one way or the other; this town has no local constable; he can get here quicker than the police from the next parish, and with more force. Go."

Siger shut the boot and stepped back; Lois got in the driver's seat, started the car, and drove out.

Siger hurried up the path to join Roy and Nancy, who had not stopped watching Siger's and Lois's attempt to find her other shoes.

And now they seemed more than a little alarmed.

"Where on earth is she going?" asked Nancy.

"To the bed-and-breakfast. We realized that is where her shoes are."

"It's not far, really," said Roy. "She could have walked."

"Yes, but she doesn't want to miss even a minute of the play."

"Well," said Roy, "I suppose we can just wait out here for her until she gets back."

"No, no, not at all. You two go in; I'll stay out here and do the watching. I mean waiting."

Roy and Nancy looked at each other as though this was a much more important decision than it should have been.

Now Siger was convinced that his theory was correct.

Roy tried to step around Siger to get a better view in the direction Lois had driven.

Siger blocked him.

"Come, come, we don't all want to miss the beginning of the play, do we?" said Siger. "The witches are the very best part!"

Roy looked again at Nancy, and then finally he said to Siger, "All right. We can come back out at the first intermission if she hasn't arrived by then. But you mustn't miss the beginning, either. We'll all go in."

"Of course," said Siger. "That's exactly what I meant."

26

They all three sat in the back, not in the front-row seats that Nancy and Roy had promised earlier.

Siger asked why, and they told him it was so that they could more easily check for Lois.

No doubt true, thought Siger. The issue was why they were so concerned about it.

Before the auditorium lights went down, Siger managed a look around at his fellow theatergoers.

The theater was filled almost to its two-hundred-person capacity. Given the size of the theater, Siger was reasonably certain that the small town's entire population of 136 was present.

Siger scanned the faces, looking for anyone who was about the same age as Laura. There were only a few. The town had mostly an older population, along with some of their grown children, in their late teens and early twenties.

It was the kind of town people would come from to start their careers and families, but not so much go to.

The footlights came on, and the director came out onto the stage to say a few words. He announced the name of a local actress taking the place of Melanie as Lady Macbeth. No mention of Laura.

Now the director left the stage and the lights went dark. Sound effects of wind and thunder began blasting, in a cheap, non-surround-sound sort of way, from two floor-size speakers to the right and left of the stage. The curtains parted and a stage spotlight came on.

"Double, double toil and trouble."

At center stage was a big papier-mâché pot painted black, and around it were gathered the three young local witches.

Siger ran through the play in his mind, trying to determine when the stage would be most dark, giving him the best chance to get out of the theater without being seen by Nancy and Roy.

If they saw him leave, he was certain they would immediately get out their smart phones and, if they got even a minimal wi-fi connection, raise a social-media alarm. The alarm wouldn't be meant for the people in the theater—they weren't in on it; at least he didn't think they were. This was not a village on the verge of a mass-hysteria event. No, the reason that the locals had all been cajoled and bullied and coaxed into the theater was so that none of them would see what was about to happen outside.

More specifically, what was about to happen on the moor—in the lower portion of it that was easily visible from just one location in the village: the pub.

It wouldn't do to wait too long. When the play was over, the pub would reopen, and most of the theater patrons would head in that direction, wanting their pints. That had to mean that the event that Roy and Nancy didn't want them to witness would then be over, as well.

And quite possibly, so would Laura Rankin's life.

Unless, of course, Siger had it all wrong. In the darkened theater, with the witches announcing schemes and predictions, while he waited for the opportunity to make his move, he had the opportunity to consider the possibility that he might have it all wrong.

Was Laura Rankin formerly Laura Penobscott, otherwise known as the Scarecrow? Certainly the yearbook proved that.

Had someone lured her to this town by writing to Sherlock Holmes and asking for the Scarecrow? Yes, that had to be the case. The letters to Sherlock Holmes were common knowledge. And anyone who followed the depictions of Baker Street Chambers in *The Daily Sun* knew both about the letters and about Laura's relationship to the QC of those chambers.

Was it connected to Laura's school twenty years ago? It had to be. Only the former teachers and pupils from that school, and in the year that Laura was there, knew the nickname Scarecrow.

So which of them had written the letter? Only three people still in town were possibilities.

There was Mrs. Hatfield, Laura's former drama teacher, who, according to the director, had had to leave on a sudden unspecified emergency.

And there was the social sciences teacher, who was not among the audience, and who had been the dance chaperone who had interrupted Laura and the future bartender on the moor. And who had made the archaeological discovery twenty years ago. The man in the yearbook photo and the man in the photo on the coroner's artifacts wall were the same; Siger was nearly sure of it.

Of course, there was also the bartender himself. Where was he? Now the scene with the witches was done, the lighting expanded onstage—and bled into the aisle where Siger was seated—with the arrival of the Scottish warlords.

Siger was angry with himself. He had probably just missed his first best chance to get out unnoticed.

He resolved not to miss the next one.

27

Laura woke to the acrid scent of something burning.

She opened her eyes. She wanted to rub them but couldn't. Rough rope chafed her wrists when she tried.

The room had gray walls. That was all she could tell from the dim candlelight some ten feet across from her.

With some effort, she sat up. The wall behind her felt cold and hard on her back.

Now she heard a voice. She couldn't see him yet; he was standing well away from the light.

"Welcome back," said Mr. Turner. "You've been out for quite a long while. We were beginning to worry. We'd hate to have to get someone new."

She didn't recognize the voice at first, as she still wasn't fully conscious. Her head was throbbing.

"Where the bloody hell am I?" she asked.

Now Mr. Turner came forward, and she could see him in the flicker of the candles, and the older couple behind him.

"You are home, in a way. As I said, welcome back."

"What do you mean, 'home'? And what stinks? Is it those candles?"

"Home because this is where you went to school. Or, more accurately, you are directly below it. And candles because they are traditional. Made of sheep fat, as you might expect. The ancient Celts didn't yet have the technology to employ the more sophisticated techniques of rendering. I'll extinguish them if they bother you, but there is something you'll want to see first."

"What?"

"In a moment. First, I must tell you this: We need your cooperation. What you did in running away was an act of highly resistant will on your part, and you put us to great trouble. First we had to rescue you from your crashed plane. That wasn't easy, since you were so limp from striking your head. You were quite lucky, of course, that the plane didn't catch on fire. But since it didn't—and since the noise of it was likely to attract attention and prompt discovery of the plane itself—we had to set fire to it ourselves. Make it appear as though you had crashed on landing, as it were. We used your necklace for that, as an identifiable object that would survive the fire. I will tell you that we considered knocking some of your teeth out as well, to match up with dental records. But such wounding in advance would have been inconsistent with the ritual. And, fortunately, I had an alternative available—Mrs. Hatfield, whose dental records were kept in the same location."

"Why . . . why are you talking about Mrs. Hatfield's dental records?"

"As I said, we need your voluntary participation. I hope now you will be persuaded to provide it."

"My voluntary participation . . . in what?"

"First things first. There's something you need to see."

"Untie me. Then you can show me anything you like. Well, within reason anyway."

He laughed and shook his head.

"You'll want to see it. Yes, there you go; I knew you could stand on your own. Turn to your left, please, and walk toward the main boiler."

Mr. Turner had a flashlight, and he flashed it briefly, high on the left wall—long enough for Laura to see rusting yellow pipes, and a half-ton heating boiler, draped in months', or perhaps years', worth of dust.

"Go on," said Mr. Turner. "What you need to see is on the floor."

Laura moved tentatively in that direction. Mr. Turner shone the light on the floor in front of her, a couple of feet at a time, just enough for her to continue.

She proceeded in that manner about ten feet.

Then, on the next move of the light, she gasped.

At her feet, below the heavy main pipe of the boiler, was Reggie.

The body of her new husband lay on the floor in front of her.

He was completely still. His eyes were closed. His legs were straight out, his arms limp.

"He is still alive," said Mr. Turner. "You can get down and take a closer look if you like."

"Untie me, you pretentious wanker."

"No."

Laura got down on her knees and leaned over Reggie.

Yes, he was still breathing. Slightly.

Eyes closed. A bloody gash on the side of his head, which had been cleaned up a bit, but not stitched, even though it clearly needed it.

She could not touch him; her hands were tied. She could not lean farther in without falling over onto him.

"Reggie," she whispered. Then: "Reggie!"

"He comes in and out of it," said Mr. Turner. "Mostly out of it. I'm not a medical professional, of course—nor is anyone who has looked at him—but I don't doubt that there might be brain swelling."

"He'll die if you leave him like this!"

"I'm sure that's true," said Mr. Turner. "And I'm sure you understand now that we are not bluffing. Neither I nor the highly devout followers whom I lead. My colleagues Roy and Nancy here delivered the letter that brought you here, and they pushed the woman into the quarry to create the need that would cause Mrs. Hatfield to ask you to stay. There might have been lesser actions that could have accomplished that of course, but a test was needed—I had to know that my lieutenants have a dedication equal to mine. And they do. When Mrs. Hatfield—useful fool that she was—realized what was happening and tried to stop it, I dispatched her entirely on my own. When it came time to deal with Charlie, I might have had difficulty, but others were already arriving to assist me. So, you understand—I have no qualms."

Laura turned to face Mr. Turner. She struggled to her feet. She contemplated just running at him, point-blank.

He saw that in her eyes, and he took a half step back, just in case.

"The point is, I need your cooperation. Medical assistance can be summoned. An anonymous phone call can be made. All that is necessary, first, is that you cooperate in doing what I ask. Which is merely to fulfill your own destiny, after all. You must come voluntarily. The stones say so. But they do not put a limit on what I can do to induce you."

Laura didn't think she should respond to that just yet.

"Where are we?" she asked.

"You don't recognize it?" said Mr. Turner. "No, I guess you would not. You were a rather mischievous girl. But more inclined, I think, to exploring the physiology of boys out on the green lawns than boiler rooms underneath school gymnasiums and the other things underground that make the world work. I suppose you didn't even know, did you, that ten feet under the blanket that you threw on the east field was the altar of a civilization that thrived three thousand years before you were born? That you desecrated it not only by your carnal presence but by memorializing that desecration in the stone itself? If there had ever been a doubt who would be the first sacrifice, it was decided at that moment, even though neither you nor I knew it yet.

"It took many years to get the translations done on the discoveries I had made—the artifacts that lay below the ground encircled by the stones. The authorities simply got in my way. Did I get a financial reward for my discovery? No. Did I receive credit for it? Nothing more than a newspaper report or two, and a brief mention on a note card in the British Museum.

"But I knew the significance of what I had found, and I acquired allies—first, among docents at the British Museum itself, and then, as the technology caught up with our needs, through both ordinary social media and then the dark web. People everywhere, of all walks of life, with one thing in common—like me, they recognized the need for a new world order to rise out of the past. So. Now, do you realize the significance of what we are about to do?"

Laura heard the question, sort of, but as a kind of

background noise, nothing more. Her head was throbbing, and she had broken a wrist, but she was not paying attention to any of that, either—but just to Reggie.

"I said," repeated Mr. Turner, "'do you realize the significance of what we are about to do?' Of what we need of you?"

Laura looked up at him.

"No, I bloody well don't. But I'll do what you ask, if you will save my husband."

"I thought you might," said Mr. Turner, and then he turned to his companions.

"Put the hood on her."

28

LONDON

Lord Buxton was staring at the Thames again. Now it was on doctor's orders; this was supposed to keep his blood pressure down. He had his doubts. For all of the years of his adult life until now, work had not been a health issue. To the contrary, from the time he was seventeen, it had been the very thing that kept him sane.

Staring at this bloody gray river would, on the other hand, most certainly drive him batty.

Without taking his eyes off the tugboat he saw chugging along toward the Tower Bridge, he reached over to his phone and punched the intercom button with a thick finger.

"Any news yet?" he demanded.

"You mean . . . regarding Laura Rankin?" said his secretary's voice.

"Of course that's what I mean."

"No," she said. "Sorry."

"What about Heath—Reggie Heath?"

"They—aren't they both supposed to be together, sir?"

"No, as a matter of fact, they are not supposed to be together. It is a universal anomaly that they are together. It's a travesty."

"Sorry, I only meant—in the sense that they are traveling together. Or at least were when they took off in that plane."

Just for a moment Buxton allowed himself the fantasy of imagining that perhaps something unfortunate had befallen Reggie but not Laura. Or, even better, that Laura had come to her senses and that was the reason for their disappearance.

That hardly made sense, though. Not given their departure in a two-seater Cessna. If something had befallen Reggie, it had almost certainly befallen Laura, as well.

That gave Buxton pause. In all of his attempts to humiliate Reggie publicly and try to make him someone hard to be with, collateral harm to Laura had never been part of the intent.

The desire to find them and make their newly wedded life problematic in any way possible had begun to fade. He had even decided not to run the pic of Reggie swinging a punch and landing in the wedding cake. Now he was wondering, Have I gone too far? Is Laura Rankin all right?

Buxton was waiting for a report from his lead paparazzo. Now, finally, the intercom buzzed.

"I have Fabio online, sir. He found one possibility. A small plane heard flying northeast through Cornwall, but no report of a landing at any of the regional airports."

"Was it identified?"

"No, sir. It was only heard, not seen. That's not much, I know."

"Get my helicopter ready."

"Yes, sir. Would you prefer *Buxton One, Buxton Two,* or *Buxton Three*?"

"Hell, I don't care. *Buxton One.*"

"Sorry, sir, but you lent *Buxton One* to the duchess of Kent."

"I did? Why?"

"So that you could track her movements, I think. But she said she'll have it back by four."

"I can't wait that long. Get *Buxton Two* ready."

"Sorry, sir, but you lent *Buxton Two* to MI6."

"Bloody hell why?"

"I believe so that they could practice locating advanced hidden tracking devices. However, they said they'll have it back by four."

"Damn. All right then, I'll take *Buxton Three.*"

"Sorry, sir, but *Buxton Three* is at the shop, having a new advanced tracking device put in. Also a new alternator."

Buxton groaned.

"Well, if they're all out, why did you even—"

"Sir?"

"Never mind. Just get a car ready. And then send *Buxton Two* to meet me in Cornwall just as soon as MI6 gets done playing with it."

"Yes, sir."

"Any idea at all where the plane was heading?"

"No, sir. The nearest town is a tiny place called Bodfyn; no airport, no constabulary, no—"

"Where did you say?"

"Bodfyn, sir."

Buxton shut off the intercom and went to look out his Thames window again.

Bodfyn. Why the hell was she going there?

There were parts of Lord Buxton's life that he rarely talked about. People who had known him within the last twelve years or so, especially those who knew him only publicly—which was the only way most knew him—thought that he had been born to be who he was now. It wasn't the case.

His family had a title and land, it was true, but no real fortune. Anyone reading his biography and noting the responsible parents and stable family life would have assumed a happy childhood, and he never bothered correcting that notion. But if anyone had asked, he could have explained that childhood isn't entirely within the control of the parents. The child's peers matter, too. Most especially at adolescence.

Bodfyn.

Lord Buxton didn't like to remember his year there at the public school. It had not been a happy one, for the most part. The glandular condition that had made him unavoidably overweight, and caused him to lag far behind all the other boys in reaching adolescence, had also caused him to go through those days under a sort of hazy mental cloud—something he himself had not even been aware of until it was gone.

Just a year and a half later, away from Bodfyn, in a new school, with a new doctor and the glandular condition finally correctly diagnosed and treated, he would have been unrecognizable to any of his original classmates. And they to him, probably, if he had ever run into any of them, which he'd never had a desire to do—with one exception.

That tall girl with the shining metal on her front teeth. Whenever he did think of Bodfyn, which was rarely, the pain in his memory of the place would come to a full stop, and then just vanish, when he remembered the sight of her at the junior winter dance. With her ungainly stance and those buckteeth.

For some years after, as he achieved one success and then another and then exponentially more, and acquired the power and women that came with all that, he wondered what had become of Laura Penobscott. He tried to imagine her grown. Surely she was nothing like the sort of women—the actresses, and models, and celebrities—that had become available to him over the past decade. But even so, at moments when it was quiet— such as looking out over the Thames—he had wondered.

And then, three years ago, it had happened. He had met Laura Rankin.

But he had met her, it seemed, just a year too late.

Now Buxton's personal secretary pinged him. He stopped looking at the Thames. His car was ready.

29

In Cornwall, a very long black limousine with a cursive *B* emblazoned in gold trim on the side pulled up at the security gate at the perimeter of Darby Manor.

The guard inside the booth noticed the emblem on the side of the vehicle, yet he did not open the gate. He came out with his clipboard, as if it were just anyone.

Lord Robert Buxton, sitting in the backseat, sighed and rolled his own window down. He knew this gate would not open—not for him—just at the request of his chauffer.

The security guard did not give an inch on the proprieties.

"Name, sir?"

"Lord Robert Buxton."

"Are you expected, sir?"

"I don't think so."

Now the guard asked something he didn't usually ask: "Do you suppose you will be welcome?"

Buxton hesitated. Then he said, simply, "Please."

Buxton watched—and waited—as the guard went back to his booth, picked up the security phone, and spoke to someone up at the house.

And then the gate opened.

The limo with the *B* went up the long drive and pulled up at the front entrance.

Spenser, the butler, was already standing there, but he did not come down the steps to open the limousine door for its passenger.

Buxton's driver started to get out to do that, but Buxton didn't wait. He got out himself and went directly up the steps to Spenser.

"I'm here to see Lady Mabel Darby."

Buxton, in both height and girth, dwarfed the skinny, slightly stooped butler with the thinning hair.

"Who shall I say is calling?" asked Spenser in a voice like cold steel.

"Lord Robert Buxton."

"Oh," said Spenser. "Wait here, please, sir, while I check."

Spenser left Buxton standing at the doorway as he went to check.

Buxton sighed. He knew that they had checked before he was allowed in the gate. He understood.

Now Spenser returned and said, "I will escort you to the terrace."

Spenser escorted Lord Buxton to the back of the house without saying another word until they reached the terrace, where Lady Mabel Darby was already having tea.

Spenser opened the door.

"Lord Robert Buxton," he announced.

Laura Rankin's aunt Mabel looked up from her tea and fixed Buxton in a glare of pale green eyes. They were shadowed and slightly bloodshot, but the stare didn't waver.

"Sit down."

Buxton did so. Aunt Mabel nodded for Spenser to leave them alone.

"What brings you, Mr. Buxton?"

Buxton swallowed hard and said, "Laura Rankin."

"Oh."

Aunt Mabel took the time to refresh her cup of tea. Only hers. She took a sip.

"You may have some tea if you like," she said now.

Buxton poured his own.

"We had visitors the other day," said Aunt Mabel. "I believe they were in your employ. Were they?"

"I am sorry," said Buxton.

"Are you aware of the things they did when they got here?"

"Yes," said Buxton.

"I rather thought you must be, given the photos that appeared in your paper."

"Again, I apologize."

"Tell me again why you are here?"

"I . . . I am concerned that none of my people has been able to find Laura Rankin."

"And you come here? To ask help of me? Indeed?"

"No, I . . . am not asking help in finding her. Wherever she is, I will leave her alone, I promise. I don't want you to tell me where she is, only that you yourself know and that all is fine. Then I will stop. I will let go. I promise."

Aunt Mabel put her cup down and looked hard at Buxton.

"Then you don't know?"

Buxton's look said that he did not.

"Her plane crashed," said Laura's aunt Mabel. "No survivors have been found."

Buxton did not respond. He stared across at Aunt Mabel, and when he made eye contact with her, Aunt Mabel saw that it was as if she had driven a sword through him.

He folded his afternoon tea napkin and put it on the table. He stood.

"I will show myself out."

Aunt Mabel shook her head.

"No," she said. "Spenser will escort you."

Outside, a two-door compact had pulled up to the gate, nearly crashing into it. The security guard recognized it, but he came out to be sure.

Lois was in the driver's seat.

"He's here, isn't he?" she said. "I called his office, I called his office, and I called his office, and his secretary finally spoke to me, and she said he was away on an urgent matter in Cornwall and couldn't speak to me, and that means he's here. Isn't he? Please tell me that he's here."

"Just so we're clear," said the guard. "Are we referring to—"

"Potty Bobby," said Lois. "Bloody Lord Robert Buxton."

30

Finally, it was time for the second appearance of the witches. Siger knew this one would be longer than the first one, and he made his move.

The moment the lights went down, he left his seat, and under the cover of that darkness he stepped up onto the far left side of the stage and then behind the heavy curtain.

The actor playing Duncan was there waiting for his cue, and he looked at Siger with some surprise. Siger put his finger to his lips and continued on backstage, sneaking quietly behind and around the wood and canvas set, until he found the back exit.

In the dark, he nearly stumbled over a stack of more or less empty paint cans and discarded one-by-fours. The sharp scent of the residual paint he'd turned loose rose up to meet him as he chose his direction. The quickest way back to the street was, of course, along the side of the building and down the nicely lit path of pavers. But that would also be within easy view of Roy and Nancy, should either of them go to the front entrance and look out.

Instead, he went twenty yards farther out from the back of the theater, to the other side of the windbreak of Scots pines. He ran along behind the screen of trees, parallel to the main street, with the pine needles crunching under his feet.

It was slow going, over an uncertain surface in the dark, and as soon as he had put a couple of small cottages with their high garden shrubs between him and the theater, he did a ninety-degree turn and cut back through one of their side yards to the street.

No one saw him committing this innocent and necessary trespass. No one was home, he knew. They were all in the theater.

Now he was on the street. Completely empty early on a Saturday night. Damp cobblestones glistened in the residual light from the lamp at the near end of the village, but his own footsteps were the only sound in the street. He worried a bit about how far that sound might carry, but he did not have the luxury of just walking to the pub.

He tried to run softly.

A light wind had sprung up, and the Wayward Pony on the pub sign rocked and squeaked as Siger reached the front of the pub. The exterior door lamp was on. He looked through the windows. No lights on inside; it was quite dark. That made sense, if the bartender had closed up and gone to the theater.

But Siger knew he hadn't arrived at the theater. The question was why.

He bent down and peered through the front window again, looking for any surface illuminated even slightly by the residual light from the outside lamp.

He saw nothing. Nothing where there should have been nothing—which is to say, on top of the clean and polished bar—but also nothing where there should have been something.

Behind the bar was a round wooden hook. Siger knew from his own time as a bartender decades ago that it was used to hang the little white towel with which the bartender wiped down the bar.

The bartender had been holding such a towel when Siger spoke to him earlier. The man had just at that moment finished cleaning up. What he would have done next was go back in and put the towel back on the hook— if he regarded it as clean enough to continue using—or replace it with a fresh one.

What he would not have done—especially if he planned on opening up again later that evening—was leave the towel hook empty.

Which it was.

The front door was double-locked, with a dead bolt.

Siger stepped back and looked around on the steps and pavement directly in front of the pub, which was the only area where there was enough light to see. It told him nothing.

But now a light gust of wind caused something to move, near the hedge at the side of the pub.

It was the bartender's white cloth, caught up in a branch.

The breeze was coming from the north. Siger proceeded in that direction, around the side, heading toward the back of the pub.

There was no light at all in back, which was a little odd. There were large lamps and heaters on the deck, and if the pub were your business, you would turn them off when not in use. But there was also a small lamp over the doorway from the pub to the deck; you wouldn't turn that one off, even when closed for the moment.

Siger reached into his coat pocket—yes, he still had the flashlight that Lois had supplied from her purse, though it was nothing more than an LED one attached to a key chain.

He shone it first at the ground in front of him. The pavement ended here; it was bare ground, sloping another twenty yards or so away from the pub, and stopping at a hedgerow—just a black silhouette in this light—that separated the civilized backyard of the pub from the moor beyond.

He turned the flashlight to his left to locate the nearest post of the deck before he bumped into it.

The post was some ten feet tall, from the sloping

ground to the level deck. Siger began to make his way just underneath the perimeter of the deck, expecting to find a set of exterior wooden steps to take him onto the deck and to the back entrance of the pub.

Except for the tiny LED light that he aimed at the ground in front of him, he was still moving in nearly pitch-black darkness.

Something gently brushed the top of his head.

Fingertips.

He knew that before even looking, and he immediately got a sick feeling at the pit of his stomach.

He aimed the light above him; saw the limp hand, arm, and shoulders draping over the edge of the deck.

He hurried forward to find the deck stairs, stumbled on the lowest one, and fell forward onto the rest. He gathered himself and hurried up the last few to the level top of the deck.

Thin glass from a broken doorway lamp crunched under his feet. He didn't think to check first for anyone else who might be standing in a dark corner. He went directly to the body that lay draped in the dark over the edge of the deck.

He felt the blood on the back of the man's head. He checked for a pulse and found none. He took a step back, used the flashlight, and recognized the bartender's face.

Now, finally, he remembered to shine the LED light around him on the deck.

Lucky, he supposed. Whoever had bashed the bartender was gone.

Now he took a more careful look.

The bartender had fallen just to one side of the coin telescope. There had been a struggle; the bartender was still in decent shape for a scrum, but he had been struck from behind by something blunt and heavy. The first blow had dazed him; the next one, to a knee, had brought him down when he'd resisted, and the third had finished him.

The bartender had clearly been taken unawares; he had not seen his assailant—or assailants—until it was too late.

And that was because he'd been looking through the telescope at the time. He had to have gone there shortly after talking with Siger earlier. He must have seen something that he was not supposed to see.

Roy and Nancy could not have done it, even if they'd had the strength. They were already at the theater.

Siger looked out from the deck. Peering into the far distance, between the two hills, he thought he saw a brief yellow-orange twinkle.

He stepped up to the telescope and looked through it. Absolutely nothing; the shutter was closed.

Bloody hell, of course. It was coin-operated. He checked, but he already knew. Did he even have any change? No. Rather embarrassing for a busker.

He checked the bartender's pockets. Yes, there was a

single pound coin. Probably the man had already used the others when he was attacked.

Siger put the coin in the telescope slot. He looked through the eyepiece, taking care not to bump it and accidentally adjust the aim.

Yes, it was already pointed directly at the narrow valley gap between the two hills.

There was the yellow-orange flicker. Then it was gone, exited stage left—but here came another flicker from the right. Now another, each of them progressing across his field of vision.

Torches. Like the one he had seen earlier, a few miles away, driving back from the school.

Siger stood. On impulse, he took a moment to pull the bartender's body fully back onto the deck. Then he took out his mobile phone.

One bar, no more. His call to Lois would not go through. He typed it in as a text instead, hoping that there might be enough of a connection for that, and then he hurried down the stairs.

Now that he knew where to look and what he was looking at, he could just barely see the glimmer of the distant torches with the naked eye.

This was what everything had been about. This view, from this place, at this time. It was the reason for the play happening on this night, and for the tremendous effort that had gone into making sure everyone would attend.

No one was supposed to see this except those who were participating.

It was the reason the bartender had been killed. He had become curious and gone to look.

The torches appeared to be about two miles away. Siger set out toward them, not running, but at the fastest walk he was capable of, which was considerable, given his long strides.

He used the tiny flashlight to the extent that he could, focusing more on where he was about to put his feet than on anything else.

This approach had its drawbacks. Straightaway, he walked into the hedge that separated the pub's land from the moor. It had been impossible to identify visually in the dark, but the sharp, nutty scent of it would have warned him if he hadn't been trying to move so quickly: The shrubs were wild yellow gorse. Bloody hell, quite literally. The flowers of those bushes are fine to look at in photos, no doubt, but try falling into one. The thorns were at least an inch in length, and now he had a dozen bloody pricks on his arms.

He continued on. He was heading for the coordinates of the archaeology find made twenty years ago, the one posted on the coroner's wall. He had memorized the topography. He knew the best route. He guessed perhaps it would take him half an hour. He hoped that would be in time.

Twenty painful minutes later, his feet bleeding inside his shoes from the repeated collisions with unseen rocks, he reached the low pass between the twin hills.

Now he could see the torches clearly. They moved right to left across the valley landscape in front of him. Some of them were coming down from a country road that ran along the north edge of the valley, some from the south. They were coming from any isolated place where the torchbearers could park their cars and proceed into the valley unseen.

If he understood the phenomenon correctly, they were coming from both town and city, from as far and unlikely a place as London itself. They were meeting in little clusters in the valley, like ants on a path to a newly discovered meal, and then proceeding, single file, along the valley creek bed to their destination.

Siger was within a hundred yards of them now. He could not go closer without being seen. But here, at least, the ground was more level, with more mud, but fewer rocks—and, though there was sufficient heather between him and the torchbearers to provide cover, some residual light from the torches filtered through. He turned off his flashlight and began to run, parallel to their procession, toward the lake.

31

Siger reached the lake. He collapsed against a tree, trying to breathe, his lungs burning—but he had gotten there first.

The wind had begun to blow clouds apart, and the half-moon was breaking through. It was just enough light to make a reflection on the water, and show the silhouette of trees on the shore. The mist on the opposite shore was rising up among the ancient oaks, even touching branches of the younger but taller Scots pines.

A yellow-orange flicker of light appeared in that mist. Then another. Then another. And then more.

Torches. Not lamps, not lanterns. Flaming torches, with dark smoke rising from the oily substances they had been soaked in. Flame, more than light. The most primitive form of dealing with darkness had reached the lake.

The first torchbearer, unrecognizable at this distance,

stepped from the forest into the water and began to cross the shallow lake.

Siger stood. Behind him, beyond the small stand of trees where he was concealed, the moor extended another half a dozen miles or more. Within the first mile was the circle of cairns dug up and exposed, along with the bones and artifacts of a culture long since dead, for the first time twenty years ago.

As he watched the torchbearers crossing the lake, Siger knew that he had gotten to the site in time, but there were more of them than he had expected.

He had no weapon. He looked on the ground for a stick, an old tree branch, anything. He knew there would be nothing when he got to the treeless site on the moor, unless he were going to just throw the stones themselves at them.

He found a dry tree branch—good for show perhaps, not much else—and he set out for the site.

He would do what he could. He hoped that Laura Rankin's fate would not depend on his debating skills, though. One thing he had never been was a politician.

32

They are just rocks in the ground, he thought.

Siger was at the site now, seated, and waiting. The clouds had now fully parted, and there was enough moonlight to see the rocks, and to see Siger sitting within the circle. When they arrived, they would have to deal with him first. He did not intend to let anyone sacrifice any virgins tonight. Or former ones, either.

They are just rocks in the ground. Oblong granite boulders, of interesting shapes to be sure, and brought here with some effort, presumably, by humankind three or four millennia ago.

Even so, just rocks. Siger found it difficult to fathom how discovering them in the modern age would instill in anyone a fascination akin to that held by inhabitants of the Bronze Age.

Was the growth of civilization irrelevant? Was the

Enlightenment for nothing, that anyone would want to go back?

Siger stood up. He looked out in the mist, and he could see the yellow flames approaching.

Well, it would be what it would be. He did not know Laura Rankin personally. By all accounts, she was someone worth defending. Then again, in circumstances such as this, anyone was.

Now they were drawing closer, beginning to assemble around him, around the perimeter of the circle, and to murmur.

At least they were close enough now that he could recognize some faces. He saw Roy and Nancy, who were looking back at him, more astonished to see him, apparently, than he was to see them.

And he saw the man he had seen in the photo in the coroner's office, and in Laura's yearbook photo, the man listed as Mr. Turner, chaperoning the dance. The hair was gray, the face thinner, but it was him.

Next to Mr. Turner stood a bound and hooded figure.

The sight of that rankled Siger. He stood, facing Mr. Turner, with the makeshift club in his hand, but not raised. If it came to that, he was in trouble.

"Remove that hood," said Siger.

Mr. Turner just looked back at him for a moment, surprised perhaps by Siger's tone under the circumstances. But he nodded to a subordinate.

"Certainly," said Mr. Turner. "She is here of her own free will, after all."

"I doubt that," said Siger.

The subordinate removed the hood.

Laura Rankin raised her head and shook it slightly, as if to rid herself of what she'd been through.

"Remove the gag, as well," said Siger.

"No," said Mr. Turner. "It was so difficult to get in place, we shall never remove it." He took a step forward, and so did all the torch-bearing men and women who were with him.

The circle grew a little tighter now. Siger could feel the heat from the torches.

"She volunteered," said Mr. Turner. "She did that when she lay in the circle of the lesser stones and allowed her initials to be carved in the rock twenty years ago. I will not now remove the gag, but if I were to do so, she would still make no objection to what we are about to do. She knows the consequences if she does."

Siger took that to mean that Heath was still alive, but he said nothing.

"It is time," said Mr. Turner now. He raised his arms toward the center of the circle, where Siger still stood. All of his acolytes followed suit, and now they began to advance.

Siger readied himself.

And then he felt a disturbance in the air—a commotion

overhead that was so loud, it was impossible to tell whether the vibrations came from the helicopter's double set of whirring blades or from the engine itself.

And now the circle was bathed in twin rings of bright white light. One light stayed on the center, and the other searched across the perimeter until it found Laura. There it stayed as Mr. Turner's followers fled in all directions.

Only Mr. Turner himself remained, defiantly holding on to Laura's arms—but only for a moment. She broke free. She turned to face him—and would have kicked him to the ground if Siger had not gotten there first.

Now the helicopter landed. The cargo doors opened, and four sharply dressed security men jumped down, with cursive *B*s on their jackets and 8mm handguns holstered to their chests.

They were superfluous now, but Siger was gratified to see them.

Even more so when Lois got out next.

33

At St. Mary's Hospital in London, there was an alert out for paparazzi. It was not an alarm, just a broadcast coded alert to the staff. Don't talk to strangers, especially if they carry cameras.

It was only a precaution. Lord Robert Buxton had given his own personal assurances that his people would respect the privacy that had been requested—and, in fact, he had offered his own security guards to enforce it—but tabloids are what tabloids do, and the hospital administrator had declined that offer.

To this point, at least, the hospital's own efforts had been successful. When Laura Rankin walked out of the lift on the third floor, she was alone. There were no pursuers with any form of media, and she was allowed to walk quietly to the Intensive Care Unit.

She entered Reggie's room. The nurse nodded and left her alone.

He was breathing on his own. Other than that, he was motionless. He had remained unconscious, as he had been when they'd returned to the school to get him. Laura had allowed no delay from the moment the helicopter had lifted off from the moor; they had gone directly to the school, and from there to here, St. Mary's.

And now there was nothing to do but wait. The blow to the head had caused an inflammation in the membrane surrounding the brain, the doctors said. It would subside. And then they would know.

She had been talking to her new husband, unconscious or no, from the moment she and Buxton's security force had retrieved him from the boiler room. Now, for this visit, she was silent. She would cry if she talked, and that might not be good. So she just put her hand on his and watched.

Now she heard someone behind her, and she turned, expecting to see the doctor.

It wasn't. It was Robert Buxton.

He stood in the doorway, uncharacteristically hesitant. She looked at him, and then turned back to Reggie, in a way that told Buxton that he could enter—or not.

He sat in the small plastic chair near the door. He waited. Laura did not look at him, but at length, she said, "Did you know? All this time, these past three years, while you courted me and tried to pry me away from Reggie, and did what you could to embarrass him and hurt his career and generally be a gigantic pain in the arse—did you know who I was?"

"Laura," began Buxton, and then he stopped and re-phrased. "Yes. Laura Penobscott. I knew from the moment I saw you again after twenty years. I saw you at the Adelphi in London and I was going backstage to be sure it was you—and I saw you leaving the theater with him. Yes, I knew it was you. I resolved to do anything that it took. I would wait for him to make a mistake—I know that he almost did once—and if he did not make one, I would do what I could to help one along."

Laura sighed.

"Do you think that is flattering?" she said. "It isn't. Well, perhaps a little, but not in a good way."

Buxton nodded.

"I am . . . extremely grateful, of course," said Laura. "And . . . well, sort of proud of you, you know, or at least . . . proud of Potty Bobby. Of everything he has become. Or at least most of it."

"That is something, I suppose," said Buxton.

"But you need to understand something," continued Laura, without turning back to look at Buxton. "I do not live in the past. People call them the 'formative years,' but I see no reason to define my life by what is said and done, by myself or others, when I've only been on the planet for a dozen years or so. There is so much after that. And however tidy it might seem—is that the right word?—however fitting it might seem that twenty years later, when Potty Bobby is on top of the world, and owns quite a lot of it, too, that I should then be his—well, it's just not how I see it. Reggie is not perfect. He is not invulnerable or all-powerful. But he loves me, and he is mine—and I stand by my choice."

Now she turned to look at him, and she saw that Robert Buxton had already gotten up and was walking away down the hall.

She smiled slightly at that, and she waited for Reggie to awaken.

34

Lois took the roundabout above Regents Park. She was in her own car now, not a rental. But she still had Siger as a passenger.

The expectation—hers anyway—was to drop him at the corner and then go to her office.

"Where are you headed?" asked Siger.

"To Baker Street Chambers, of course," said Lois. "To hold down the fort until Reggie recovers. Or Nigel returns. Or . . . whatever."

"I'll go along with you." Siger nodded.

Lois wasn't sure what he meant.

"You . . . aren't part of chambers," she said as nicely as possible.

He looked hurt.

"Unless you're going to tell me now that you used to be a barrister."

"No. I wasn't."

"Or a solicitor."

"No. Not that, either."

"Or a law chambers clerk—but that's my job, you know."

"No, I haven't been any of those things."

"Oh," said Lois. She laughed. "You've been in almost every line of work we've encountered. I'm a little surprised."

She hoped he couldn't tell that she was also just a little disappointed.

"No, I'm afraid I've not been any of those things."

He paused, and they took the turn onto Baker Street in silence.

"I was a detective once, though."

They had reached the Marylebone car park now. They both got out of the car and walked up the two hundred block of Baker Street. They paused at the doorway of Baker Street House.

"Well . . ." began Lois.

"I'll just come in, too, if you don't mind. There's someone on the top floor I need to have a word with."

"There's no one on the top floor except Mr. Rafferty. And the board of directors."

"Yes," said Siger as he held the door for Lois. "That is correct."

As they entered the lobby, the lift had just now descended; the lift doors opened, and Rafferty stepped out.

"Ah, here he is now," said Siger.

Lois got into the lift. She looked back at Siger, saw that he was remaining in the lobby with Rafferty, and gave him a wave.

"Cheers," said Siger, waving back as the lift doors closed.

Rafferty had been on his way out, but Siger detained him in the lobby.

"You know," said Siger, "you might throw some money in my violin case now and then."

"As if you really need it," said Rafferty slyly, but then Siger gave him a look.

"Sorry," said Rafferty. "I'm always in such a rush in the morning, you know."

"Yes, I know."

"Well. Do you want me to convene the committee? I know the Heaths have had some difficulty managing lately."

"No," said Siger. "That's what I dropped by to tell you. We will keep the Baker Street lease in place. I've looked into it, and I have confidence in our current occupant."

"Excellent. Well then. Good day, Mr. Sigerson."

"Good day, Mr. Rafferty."